THE MYSTERY OF BILTMORE HOUSE

Published by Gallopade International/Carole Marsh Books. Printed in the United States
of America.

Acknowledgements: the photography for the cover of this book was used with permission from The Biltmore Company, Asheville, North Carolina.

Also available:
The Mystery of Biltmore House Teacher's Guide

Gallopade International is introducing SAT words that kids need to know in
each new book that we publish. The SAT words are bold in the story. Look
for this special logo beside each word in the glossary. Happy Learning!

Gallopade is proud to be a member and supporter of these educational organizations
and associations:

American Booksellers Association
American Library Association
International Reading Association
National Association for Gifted Children
The National School Supply and Equipment Association
The National Council for the Social Studies
Museum Store Association
Association of Partners for Public Lands
Association of Booksellers for Children
Association for the Study of African American Life and History
National Alliance of Black School Educators

Once upon a time...

Papa said ...

Why don't you set the stories in real locations?

That's a great idea! And if I do that, I might as well choose real kids as characters in the stories! But which kids would I pick?

MiMi, PiCK ME, PiCK ME!

ME, TOO, MiMi, PiCK ME, TOO!

Christina

Grant

Pick Me!

6

On the *Mystery Girl* airplane ...

I can FLY US anywhere!

Or aboard the *Mimi!*

Take me to the Forbidden City!

Or by surfboard, rickshaw, motorbike, camel ...

All great ideas! I can put a lot of history, MYSTERY, legend, lore, and laughs in the books! We can use other boys and girls in the books. It will be educational and fun!

Good stuff!

Where will you get the other kids, Mimi?

From my Fan Club! Kids can apply to be characters!

And can you put some cool stuff online? Like a Book Club and a Scavenger Hunt and a Map so we can track our adventures?

Of course!

And can cousins Avery and Ella and Evan and some of our friends be in the books?

Of course!

Can I apply?

and so, Mimi, Papa, Christina, and Grant took off aboard the Mystery Girl and America's National Mystery Book Series—where the adventure is real and so are the characters! —was born.

START YOUR ADVENTURE TODAY!

Stacy Brown   **Trent Thompson**   **Wendy Longmeyer**   **Michael Marsh**

ABOUT THE CHARACTERS (30 YEARS AGO)

Stacy Brown, age 11, lives in Asheville, North Carolina. She really does show dogs and play bridge!

Trent Thompson, age 10, lives in the Greenville-Spartanburg, South Carolina area.

Wendy Longmeyer has previously appeared in *The Secret of Somerset Place* and will be a character in *The Great Clemson Football Mystery*.

Michael Marsh, age 10, is the author's son. He lives in Tryon, North Carolina, and is Vice President of Gallopade Publishing Group.

Special Appearances by Bob Terrell, Asheville Citizen Times, *Kevin McKee, WLOS-TV, Jim McAllister,* Greenville News-Piedmont, *and the* Spartanburg Daily Herald's *"Stroller."*

Stacy and Trent in the Winter Garden

1
FOUR HOT, SWEATY, CRAZY, MAD KIDS

Stacy Brown dealt the cards into the sloppy stacks in the back seat of the red station wagon. She snapped each card with as loud a pop as she could. She was mad.

"That sure doesn't sound like homework," her mom commented from the front seat.

Snap. "School's". . . *pop* . . ."out," Stacy reminded her.

Her mom mumbled and Stacy mumbled back. School was out, and all of her friends were starting their part-time summer jobs. All except her. And here she was stuck in Asheville on her way to Biltmore House where she had been a hundred . . . thousand . . . million times before. Just because her mom had to help coordinate a mystery writing workshop being held at the estate this week.

Stacy had a part-time job at a kennel all lined up. She needed money badly. There was an international dog show in California, where she used to live, the next week. And, boy, did she want to go. Shoot, she'd been showing dogs since she was a puppy herself. She'd won lots of prizes. But this worldwide meet would be just wonderful. The time was right. It was for kids just her age, thirteen. And her dog was in perfect condition.

Her mom always said you have to make things happen. So Stacy had worked hard to get that job to make enough money to go. But now her mom was making her tag along with her like she was a baby or something.

Next to showing dogs, Stacy's favorite thing was playing bridge. But it didn't seem like much fun today in the hot, sweaty back seat playing all four hands by herself.

Stacy saw her mom look at her in the rearview mirror. *Spy*, Stacy thought. I'm being watched. She could see her mom frown at her windblown hair and her skirt that was wrinkled from sprawling in a not too ladylike position, trying to make room for invisible bridge partners. Stacy turned her face where her mom couldn't see it and made an awful face.

Why did they have to meet the others here at historic Biltmore Village? Why couldn't they have met them at the McDonald's across the street where they had civilization — milk shakes?

The blue Mustang sped down I-26 toward the mountains. He's gonna get a ticket, the boy in the back seat thought. He stared up into the sky looking for a blue light to come from outer space and pull them over. Nothing. Shucks.

Trent Evans swiped a thin streak of perspiration above his lip. "Air," he moaned dramatically from the back seat. "Air!"

He pretended he was being kidnapped and held hostage. Didn't that happen recently somewhere between Spartanburg and Asheville? Any minute he was going to be tossed in the trunk where summer had been stored since last year. Maybe his dad could put that in a mystery story.

Somehow, while all his friends were heading the opposite direction, toward the cool South Carolina coast, he was trapped into going with his dad to a writing workshop in Asheville.

He didn't even know his dad wanted to be a writer. He wasn't a writer. He was an engineer. But the textile plant he worked for had some temporary layoffs. His dad was always telling him when life gives you lemons, make lemonade. And so he had decided that instead of moping around the house worrying about lost hours, he would try his hand at writing.

Trent was sure it had all been his mother's idea. He knew that it had been her idea that this would be a great time for father and son to get to know each other better.

Trent sank back into the hot cushion and watched the mountains get larger before his very eyes. "I'll bet I could get to know Dad real good at the beach," he muttered. "Besides, if you don't know your dad by the time you're eleven, when are you supposed to know him?"

Wendy and Michael Hunt sat glumly in the back seat of the car. They were both hunched over some of Mother's long pads of yellow paper. Michael was inventing a new video game where a horrid monster gobbled up big sisters. Wendy was writing notes about which cute fourth grade girl Michael was in love with to pay him back.

Suddenly, the car swerved left, then right, tossing their papers out of their hands. Mother never takes the straight route, Wendy thought. We could have gotten on the interstate and made it from Tryon to Asheville in thirty minutes. But if there was a long way around, Mother always took it.

Mother's camera equipment and trusty rusty typewriter were piled up on the seat beside her. She never went anywhere without either one. "A tornado might come charging down the road and I wouldn't want to miss it," she would always say. I can just picture her making a picture of us getting scooped up by some big black inverted triangle, Wendy thought.

Michael was mad, too. It had been his turn to ride in the front. But they had argued about it and so Mother had pointed them both to the back seat. It was going to be a long, hot summer, he decided. And what a way to start — going to a big, old house so his mother could attend a writing workshop. She'd written a bunch of books — why did she need more courses, he wondered. Then he remembered. She wasn't taking a class, she was teaching one. As if being a mother weren't bad enough, now she was going to be a teacher, too. The thought of the combination gave him cold chills up his hot backbone.

At precisely the same time, two cars whipped into the steaming asphalt parking places beside Stacy's car. A white car on the left; a blue one on the right. She felt like she was in the middle of a twelve-wheeled American flag. A fast glimpse showed her there was one boy in one car and a boy and girl in the other. A foursome for bridge, she thought. Then she frowned. They probably didn't like cards. They probably won't like me. And I'll bet they don't want to be here any more than I do.

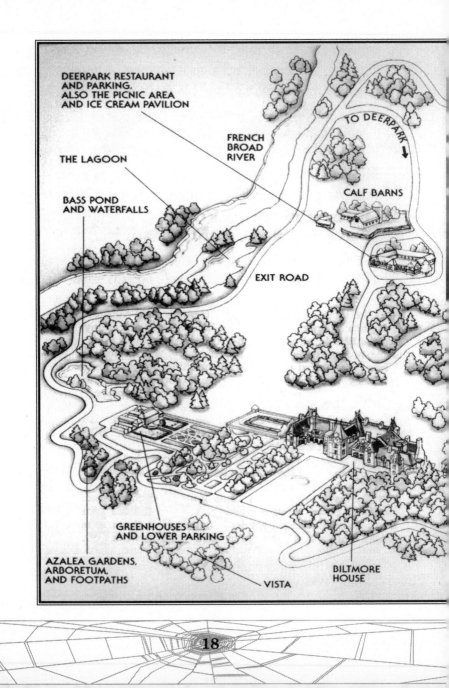

DEERPARK RESTAURANT
AND PARKING,
ALSO THE PICNIC AREA
AND ICE CREAM PAVILION

FRENCH
BROAD
RIVER

TO DEERPARK

THE LAGOON

CALF BARNS

BASS POND
AND WATERFALLS

EXIT ROAD

GREENHOUSES
AND LOWER PARKING

AZALEA GARDENS,
ARBORETUM,
AND FOOTPATHS

VISTA

BILTMORE
HOUSE

BILTMORE HOUSE & GARDENS

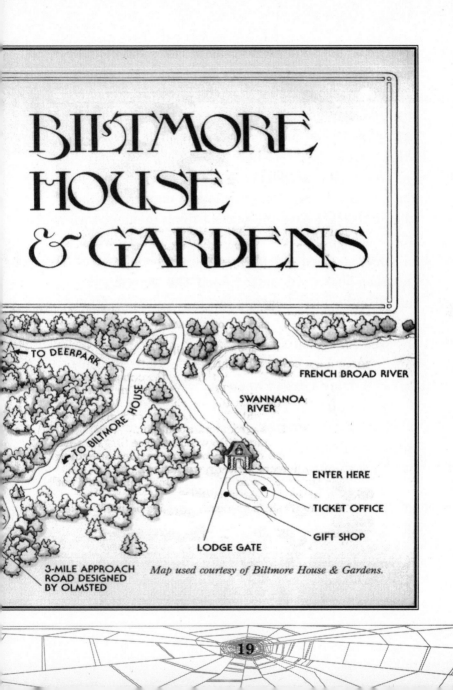

← TO DEERPARK

TO BILTMORE HOUSE

FRENCH BROAD RIVER

SWANNANOA RIVER

ENTER HERE

TICKET OFFICE

GIFT SHOP

LODGE GATE

3-MILE APPROACH ROAD DESIGNED BY OLMSTED

Map used courtesy of Biltmore House & Gardens.

The adults all hopped out of the cars and met on the sidewalk. Stacy could tell from the nodding and shaking of hands that introductions were being made all around. The kids just sat in the cars and stared meanly at one another, as though it was the others' fault they were here.

The adults chuckled. As her mom got back in the car, Stacy heard her say loudly enough for the kids to hear, "I have the perfect thing to cheer this hot bunch up before we head for Biltmore House."

Stacy scooped all her cards into a pile and stacked them up in record time. As if she was jumping hurdles, she bounded over the seats into the front one beside her mom. She knew what that meant.

Trent stared at the crazy girl in the car next to him. He was puzzled by her hopping around. Then he was even more puzzled when she waved gaily at him.

Wendy and Michael looked through the steamy window at the strange girl in the next car. She turned and smiled at them. "Whatever she's got to be happy about is a mystery to me," Wendy muttered.

Spreading the tips of his fingers up to the edge of the window, Michael waved and smiled back at the mysterious-acting girl.

2

FOUR FRIENDS, FOUR SURPRISES, ONE MYSTERY

Like a red, white and blue streamer, the cars left Biltmore Village and its quaint little shops with funny names like Mudpies. They cut across the busy intersection, ignoring the entrance to Biltmore House. Then they pulled up to a brick building and stopped.

Stacy hopped out eagerly and motioned for the others to hurry up. "You're going to love this place," she said.

Before she could even get a chance to tell them she was Stacy Brown, her mom steered them into the Biltmore Dairy Bar.

"We already had lunch," Wendy grumbled as the waitress ushered them to a cheerful green and yellow booth.

"At least the cool air feels good," Michael said, plopping down on the cushion. Wendy shoved him over. Stacy and Trent sat down across from them. The adults chose a table nearby and with a wink from Ms. Brown ordered seven specialties of the house.

Trent yawned. He pulled a Rubik's cube from his pocket and began to twist it in a bored manner.

"That thing's no fun," Stacy said.

"It's not fun," Trent argued. "It's hard.

"Hard!" said Stacy. "You try bridge. Bridge is hard."

"Shoot," said Wendy. "Bridge is easy. We play every time my sister Michele is home . . ."

"And we can twist our mother's arm to be the fourth," Michael butted in. "Besides, bridge isn't hard. Now take chess," he said. "Every time I try to castle . . ."

"What's castle!" asked Stacy. "You mean like Biltmore House?"

"Biltmore House is not a castle," Wendy argued. "Is it?"

"Sure," said Stacy. "Wait till you see it. You'll agree it's a castle all right."

"So what," said Trent, twisting the cube faster and faster into a blur of blue. "The only castle I'm interested in is a sand castle—at the beach."

"Me, too." "Yeah!" they cheered, and grinned to find themselves in agreement about something.

"Well," said Stacy. "Do we also agree that we wish our parents were doing something besides attending this stupid mystery writers' workshop?"

"We sure are," said Wendy. "Only, our mom's not taking classes . . . she's teaching them."

"You mean she's written mysteries before?" asked Trent.

"Sure," said Michael. "Lots of them, and I help her."

"*Suuuure*," Stacy said.

"He's not kidding," Wendy said. "We always go with her when she does her research for a mystery book."

Michael put his elbows on the table and laid his head in his hands. "And we always get mixed up in a real-life mystery ourselves," he groaned.

"Hey," said Trent. "That sounds like fun."

"Well," said Wendy thoughtfully. "Sometimes. But not when you get accused of stealing pirate's heads . . . or beating up beasts . . . or . . ."

"But remember," Michael said, "Mother said no mystery this time. She promised. She's teaching—not writing."

"Maybe my dad will have her for a class," Trent said. "I wouldn't mind if he wrote mysteries if I got to meet a pirate and stuff like that."

"Aw, it gets boring after awhile," Wendy said.

They all howled with laughter.

"Sure," said Stacy. "What's one more dead body?"

"Yeah," said Trent, waving his fingers spookily in the air. "Or a couple of extra ghosts."

Then suddenly, just as if a ghost had appeared, the kids all hushed at once. In the center of the table, appearing like magic, were four of the most enormous chocolate sundaes any of them had ever seen.

"Look at that!" Trent finally said.

"Yikes," moaned Wendy. "The calories!"

"Can I have anyone's whipped cream and cherry?" Michael begged.

Stacy thrust her long silver spoon deep into a mound of hot fudge sauce. "I told you you were going to like this place."

"Do you get to come here often?" Wendy asked.

"Oh, sure," Stacy said. "Every time we go to Biltmore House."

"Biltmore . . . Biltmore . . . Biltmore . . . ," Michael muttered. "That's all I've heard for days."

"Well, if it weren't for the dairy cows at the Biltmore estate, you wouldn't be enjoying this luscious sundae," Stacy warned him.

"You mean they have a chocolate sundae factory there?" Michael asked.

"No, silly," Stacy sputtered. "They have one of the largest dairy farms anywhere. That was part of Mr. Vanderbilt's plan."

"Who is Mr. Vanderbilt?" Trent asked, looking around the room.

"He's the man who built Biltmore House," Stacy explained. "He wanted it to be self-sufficient."

"You mean have everything he needed right there on the estate?" Trent asked.

"Something like that," said Stacy.

"Our parents are always trying to get us to be self-sufficient," Michael said.

"Independent," Wendy agreed between mouthfuls. "Nothing happens unless you make it happen, Mom always says."

"Well, that was what Mr. Vanderbilt thought too," Stacy said. "He made Biltmore happen."

"Well, I'm sure glad he made these chocolate sundaes happen," Trent said.

Then there was silence as they each stuffed heaping spoonfuls of ice cream into their mouth. At the next table they could hear the adults talking excitedly about the upcoming writing workshop.

They sound just like kids at the lunchroom table at school — laughing, talking, and cutting up, and teasing each other, Stacy thought. Her mom was teasing Wendy's and Michael's mother that she couldn't solve a real mystery.

Then, suddenly, each of their spoons stopped halfway between their mouths and the tall tulip dishes dripping with chocolate as Stacy's mother leaned forward and whispered loudly — "Speaking of mysteries, listen to what I heard this morning."

The other adults leaned in closer; the children listed sideways toward the table.

"What is she saying?" Trent asked.

"Can't hear her," Stacy said.

Michael and Wendy watched their mother listen eagerly and nod. Michael's spoon clanged as he dropped it on the table. "Uh, oh," he said.

"No mystery!" Wendy hissed. "She promised!"

3

ONE CREEPY CASTLE, ONE SCARY QUESTION

By the time they finished cleaning up Michael's mess, the adults had paid the check and left. Quickly the kids followed.

"Let's all go in my car," Stacy's mom volunteered. "Maybe I can tell you a little bit about the house before we get there."

Everyone piled into the station wagon. The adults got comfortable in front. The kids crammed into the back. They passed a sign that said "Biltmore Forest." Stacy still remembered the first time she had seen that sign after she had learned to read. It had made her think of fairy tales and princesses and dragons and long ago and far away and happily-ever-afters. It still did.

In just a few minutes they were at the Lodge Gate. Ms. Brown slowed down and stopped. A serious, uniformed guard greeted them.

"Afternoon," he said sternly. "Your tickets, please?" Even though he said it as a question, it always sounded to Stacy like he meant you'd-better-have-your-tickets-or-else-off-to-the-dungeon or something like that.

"We're here for the writers' workshop," Ms. Brown informed him. Slowly he stalked back to the gatehouse desk and checked their names off a list. He looked suspiciously at the kids in the back, and Stacy wondered if they would have to get out and walk or something.

But the man stepped backwards and hoisted a stiff arm into the air indicating they could pass. Slowly, Ms. Brown began the long drive to the largest castle in America.

Stacy had ridden down this road a hundred times, but to the others it was new. They stretched and strained their necks in the crowded back seat to see what they could see.

The road was a winding lane curving through a deep forest. Twisting past mirrorlike pools and tinkling streams and waterfalls, it always made Stacy feel like she had opened up a book of fairy tales and was driving right into the first page. She was certain that if elves and trolls were real, they would live beneath the moss-covered rock walls.

"They call this the Approach Road," Ms. Brown said quietly.

"The woods seem so . . . so neat," Mr. Evans said.

"That's because they tend this area," Ms. Brown told him.

"All this?" Trent said from the back seat.

Stacy wondered if he had to help with yard work at home like she did. "It was part of Mr. Vanderbilt's plan," she said. "Like I told you."

They were all silent. Stacy listened. She couldn't help but think how unusual it was for a group of people to be together and just be quiet. It was sort of neat, like it gave them all something in common.

She wished she could read everyone's mind. Were the adults writing mysteries in the minds? Were the kids deciding a visit to Biltmore might not be so bad after all?

She thought about how boring it was to come here after awhile, and yet now she felt really proud that she could tell the others about this place that was practically in her backyard.

It seemed like there was one of every living plant on the estate. Thick-leafed rhododendrons made great umbrellas to hide under. Her uncle made walking sticks from the wavy-stemmed mountain laurel. Tulip poplars towered overhead; light-laced wildflowers tickled underfoot.

She started to tell them how pretty the Approach Road was in the spring when the pink azaleas bloomed, or in the winter when the spruces hung low with snow over the winding path. But the curvy ride through the ravines and ridges made her a little dizzy and drowsy. She felt like she could fall asleep in the back of the warm car. Then something startled her.

"Yikes!" Michael squealed.

After the **meandering** three-mile ride, they had finally come around the last turn and through the tall iron gates and pillars topped by stone sphinxes.

The other kids began to whistle and talk at once. "There's a castle hiding up here in the woods," Wendy said.

"It's a whole town," Trent insisted.

"It's a mansion," Michael said.

Stacy and the adults laughed. She guessed she had forgotten how she felt the first time she saw it herself. "That is Biltmore House!"

Ms. Brown stopped the car and everyone stumbled out for a look.

"You kept saying *house*," Wendy said to Mother.

"Yeah," said Michael. "You know, like three bedrooms, a couple of baths, maybe a deck."

Everyone laughed.

Stacy looked up proudly at the huge house as though it were her own. Majestically it stood at the end of a long, narrow, grassy lawn lined by rows of fluffy green poplar trees. In the shimmering heat of the summer day the pinkish walls and blue roof pointing up into the sky almost looked like a **mirage** — as if it were floating in midair like a dream or something you only thought you saw.

"Does Mr. Vanderbilt actually live here?" Trent asked, stretching out on the cool grass.

"No one lives here now," Ms. Brown said. "But Mr. George Washington Vanderbilt built the house around a hundred years ago for his family. He copied the house after a French chateau."

"What's that?" whispered Michael.

Stacy giggled. She had already figured out that Michael's whispers were as loud as some kid's talking. Ms. Brown overheard him. "It's a French word for house."

"Or castle," added his mom.

"See," said Wendy. "I told you it was a castle."

"No one has argued with that," said Mr. Evans.

"It must have cost a lot of money," Trent said.

"Let's just say Mr. Vanderbilt had a lot of money," said Ms. Brown.

"If he had so much money, why did he build such a swanky joint here instead of France or New York or Hawaii?" Wendy asked.

Mother frowned. "What could be more beautiful than the Land of the Sky?" she asked.

"He liked the mountains just like we all do," said Stacy.

"Also, like I heard Stacy telling you at lunch," Ms. Brown said, "Mr. Vanderbilt wanted his family to be able to live off the estate." She pulled a pale blue brochure from her pocket and unfolded it. "See," she said. "Here are the farms and the gardens and the dairy and the vineyards." She pointed to different places on the map.

"You mean they didn't have to run down to the Fast Fare all the time for milk and bread?" Michael said.

Everyone howled. Trent rolled over and over in the grass.

"You might say that," Ms. Brown agreed.

"Well I wish we were more that way now," Mother said. "So we weren't so dependent on others for just the necessities of life."

"Like a soft drink," Michael said, swiping at his sweaty forehead. The adults just ignored him and wandered off to look at what Stacy told them was the "Rampe Douce" — a series of slanted walkways that led up to the Statue of Diana and a super view of the house.

Wendy fell down on the grass beside Trent. "I'll pass on that view," she said.

"I'm glad I don't have this paper route," Michael muttered, and Trent went into another series of giggles.

"I'm glad I'm not the maid," Wendy moaned.

"Or the grass cutter," added Trent.

Stacy couldn't help but feel a little offended that they made fun of the house. After all her griping about having to come up here again, she didn't like the idea of anyone not thinking it was a really neat place.

But before she could complain, the kids grew quiet. They stared at Wendy staring at the house. Slowly she looked over it from one end to the other, her eyes following the pointed spires.

"What is it?" Michael asked.

"What do you see?" demanded Trent.

Stacy figured Wendy was just trying to be a smart aleck.

Wendy absentmindedly scratched at a mosquito bite on her knee.

"I was just thinking," she said, "that it looks sort of like a castle in Transylvania."

"You mean Dracula's castle!" Trent said.

Stacy could have sworn he shivered even in the hot sunlight.

"Just picture it at night with a full moon hovering over it," Wendy said.

"Aw, you've just been around mystery writers too long," Stacy said, but not very convincingly. She had been here at night, and it was sort of scary.

"It does look like it might have a tower and a dungeon," Trent said.

Wendy turned to Stacy. "Is it haunted?" he demanded.

"No," said Stacy. "Of course not."

"No skeletons in the closet?" asked Trent.

"How should I know?" said Stacy. "There's a million closets in the place."

Suddenly Michael's blue eyes got very big and he looked up at the house and then at Stacy. "I just have one question," he said. "We're not spending the night in there, are we?"

4
TWO SPOOKY PLACES TO SPEND THE NIGHT

Stacy couldn't help herself. For just a minute she was deadly quiet. Just long enough for Michael and the others to believe that they were going to spend the night in the big, brooding castle. She had never even thought of Biltmore House as scary. But their talk was giving her second thoughts.

Finally she said, "No."

The others frowned at her. She waved a hand at them to wait a minute and hear her out. "I was just thinking," she said. "We're not staying here . . . we're staying at the Grove Park Inn."

"Oh, that sounds better," Wendy said.

"Sure does," the boys agreed.

Stacy shook her head. "Not really," she said very seriously. "That place is really scary!"

"Why?" asked Michael.

Stacy just shook her head. She couldn't put it into words. They would just have to see for themselves.

The adults had wandered back down the Rampe Douce and motioned for the kids to come to the car.

"I want to go in the castle," Wendy moaned.

The others glared at her in surprise. For the last hour she had complained about coming to Biltmore.

"I want to go to Grove Park and see why Stacy thinks it's so scary," Michael said.

Trent lagged behind them, taking very long, slow steps. "I want to go to a very unmysterious, not scary McDonald's for some absolutely unfrightening French fries," he said.

"Keep your eyes on your fries," Michael said spookily, pulling his tee shirt up over his mouth and nose, elbow stuck out, Dracula style.

"We'll come back in a little while," Ms. Brown assured them. "I want to show you the rest of the estate."

"And we've got to get over to Grove Park and get checked in," Mr. Evans said, looking at his watch.

"Yes," said Ms. Hunt. "I have to register my students so we can get back here for the get-together party tonight."

Stacy dove into the back of the station wagon head first as though the quicker she got in the quicker they could go and get back.

The others followed, and Ms. Brown pulled back onto the winding lane. Again, everyone was entranced by the beautiful grounds all around the house.

"It looks like even the weeds have been landscaped," Trent said.

"Believe me they are," said Ms. Hunt. "Remember that article I did about gardens?" she asked. Wendy and Michael both shook their heads *no*. "Well," she said. "I remember telling you about a man named Frederick Law Olmsted. He designed Central Park in New York City."

"Oh, yes," said Wendy with a grin. "We wanted you to take us to see it."

"That's right," Michael added. "The marathon runs and the zoo."

"And the muggings," said Wendy.

Their mother ignored them. "Well, that's the same man Mr. Vanderbilt hired to lay out Biltmore's gardens."

Just as she said that, they came around a curve and some of the gardens appeared before them like another fairy tale. Even from here they could see that the gardens were laid out in neat patterns.

Narrow paths wound between the shapes. Through the middle of the garden there was a long, latticed walkway covered with grapevines.

Ms. Brown drove the car through the gateway of the walled garden. Stacy felt like she was in *The Secret Garden*, which had been her favorite book for years and years.

"This is the finest English garden in America," Mr. Evans said.

Stacy looked closely but she couldn't figure out what made it English or German or Australian.

"Walled gardens were used to trap sunshine and stop cold wind," Mr. Evans explained. "So it made a better place for flowers to grow year 'round."

Stacy believed him. Red and blue and yellow flowers bloomed everywhere.

They passed a rose garden that Ms. Brown said had over 2,000 rose bushes in it.

At the end of the garden was a big glass-topped greenhouse that Ms. Hunt called a **conservatory.**

"Can we stop?" Trent begged.

"Not today," Ms. Brown said.

"You kids can visit here tomorrow while we're having class," Ms. Hunt added.

But Trent just looked wistfully out the back window. Stacy figured he and his dad must really have a thing about flowers.

Soon they passed an even more tempting place to stop — the Bass Pond. A footbridge crossed a large waterfall at one end. The rocky pools and bubbling streams looked cool and inviting.

But Stacy moaned to herself. *Tomorrow.* Why did it always seem like everything was always tomorrow? Good things like vacation and allowance and birthdays were always tomorrow, and everything not so hot like homework and chores and tests were always today.

They rode past the Lagoon and followed the blue waters of the French Broad River for awhile. Then they were at the calf barn.

"Is this where the makings of those neat chocolate sundaes come from?" Michael asked.

"I guess you could say the beginning," Ms. Brown said. "In fact, in many ways this was the beginning of Mr. Vanderbilt's ideas about Biltmore. He wanted to use the land for its best benefit and thought farming and dairying would do well here. At first the Biltmore herd was just to supply the Vanderbilt family, their guests and workers with milk and cheese and cream. But it was so delicious that before long they opened a dairy and it's still around today."

"I'm sure glad," Michael said.

"Mr. Vanderbilt was pretty smart, wasn't he?" Stacy asked.

"He sure was," her mom said. "He wanted to make things happen. And the only way they do is for you to dig right in and make them happen."

Stacy frowned. That's what her mom had said about her going to the dog show in California. Stacy would have to earn her own money for an airplane ticket if she wanted that to happen. But she didn't have lots of money like Mr. Vanderbilt. And she bet Mr. Vanderbilt never wanted to be a mystery writer.

Next they passed a place that looked like another dairy barn. But Ms. Brown called it Deerpark. Trent craned to see if he could see any deer.

Ms. Brown looked in the rearview mirror and saw him. "Not now," she said. "But this did used to be a deer preserve. Now it's a restaurant. I'm sure we'll get a chance to eat here sometime this week."

Tomorrow, Stacy thought again, beginning to feel like she was trapped in a time warp car with no way to get out until tomorrow — only it never was tomorrow.

As they headed through the hilly streets of town towards the Grove Park Inn, the adults talked excitedly about taking a writers' workshop here in Asheville.

"Why does that make it so special?" Wendy asked.

"Well," her mother said. "Just think of all the great writers who have lived around Asheville — like Thomas Wolfe."

"And O. Henry," Ms. Brown added. "I just love him."

"And how about Carl Sandburg?" Mr. Evans said, in admiration. "He lived nearby at Flat Rock."

"I didn't even know there was a flat rock around," Wendy said, looking out at the mountains.

"Who are all those people?" Wendy asked.

At once the adults began to moan and groan just like kids do when someone says something they can't believe like, "Who's that rock group?"

"If you kids don't know who those famous writers are, you need to," Ms. Hunt insisted.

Uh oh, thought Stacy. This is beginning to sound too much like school.

"You *have* to learn who they are," Mr. Evans agreed.

"Does anyone want to go back to Biltmore Dairy Bar?" Ms. Brown asked pleasantly. All the children hooted yes except Stacy, who waited.

"Then tell me who those writers are we were just talking about and when you do I'll take you," she said.

The car was silent with disappointment. But only for a moment. Ms. Brown had pulled into a shaded drive where the sun seemed to have vanished. A big stone building like the seven dwarves' house pumped up with air appeared before them.

"Oh no," said Michael. "You weren't kidding. This is spookier than ever!"

5
LOTS OF WEIRD PEOPLE

The huge old hotel looked like a big, lumpy, stone monster about to gobble them up through it wide-mouthed doors.

The unusual walls of the Grove Park Inn looked like they were made of smooth boulders stacked upon one another. Even though nothing seemed to hold them together, the rocks looked like nothing could cause them to tumble down.

A wavy, red-tiled roof hung low over the wide porch. Draped over the roof were the low-hanging limbs of sad-looking fir trees.

It felt several degrees cooler in the shadow of the building. Except for an old man in a white coat who did not move, there did not seem to be anyone around.

"*This* is where we are going to stay?" Wendy asked.

"Looks neat to me," Michael said with that ready to explore no-matter-what-mom-says look in his eye.

"This is one of the nicest old inns I know of," Ms. Hunt said. "I want you all to behave while we're here."

"Yes," said Mr. Evans. "You'll be on your own for awhile."

Trent nodded seriously at his father, then turned and winked at the others. "Yes sir! I mean yessir," he said trying hard not to giggle.

"That's right," said Ms. Brown thoughtfully as they unloaded suitcases. "Remember, there are a lot of things to be careful about, both here and at Biltmore House. You don't want to get into any trouble."

Stacy figured she meant for them not to break anything, like a valuable antique or some old person's leg, by running through the lobby. But she couldn't help but think about what they had overheard earlier — or rather had not quite overheard — at the dairy bar. Was there more trouble to stay out of than they suspected?

There wasn't time to ask or even think about it now. A man lugging two metal luggage carts behind him appeared from nowhere and began to help them load their suitcases and typewriters and tennis rackets. When the carts were filled, he dragged them just as if they were still empty into the hotel.

The adults followed him and the kids followed them. Once they were inside, it felt like the temperature had dropped another ten degrees, it was so cool. The adults headed for the registration desk to check in. But Stacy and the others just stood there and looked around, their mouths hanging open.

The lobby was so big that it looked like an entire house would fit into it. The ceilings were high, and huge chandeliers hung down.

Scrambling in different directions, they investigated the unusual hotel.

"This sure isn't like a Holiday Inn," Trent said.

"This isn't like any inn where I've ever stayed," Wendy said.

"Look at this!" Michael yelled from across the room.

They ran toward him. There he stood, looking like a little elf, in the biggest fireplace they had ever seen. There was another one just like it at the other end of the lobby. It was so tall that even a grownup could walk inside it. The logs laid out for the evening fire were really small trees.

And then when they thought they had seen everything, the adults called to them. They ran to catch up, and they found them waiting patiently by a small door in the seven dwarf-like wall. Suddenly, the door shuddered and opened. It was an elevator!

It seemed like it was forever before they got unpacked and dressed for dinner. Stacy decided it would really be pretty neat to spend the week exploring all these big old houses. Michael and Wendy's mother had even told them she might take them to see Thomas Wolfe's house.

At last her mom was ready, and they joined the others in the lobby. By then the fires were blazing brightly. They really felt good in the big, cool room — even on a summer's night.

While the writers and would-be-writers got acquainted, Stacy walked out on the big patio that ran all across the back of the hotel. The sun had almost set over the mountains which encircled the city. The bluish-pink light gave everything a lonesome look. Of course, this time of day always gave Stacy a funny feeling in her stomach. Sort of sad. Maybe a little creepy.

Michael charged out onto the patio. "You should come and meet some of these weird people," he said.

"They're just a bunch of writers," Wendy said.

"Well, some of them look more like characters in a mystery story than mystery story writers to me," said Trent. "There's a guy who looks like Edgar Allan Poe," he added.

Michael looked puzzled.

"You know," said Wendy. "The poet who wrote all the scary mystery stories and poems."

"Yeah," said Stacy. "One time I even memorized *The Raven*."

"You did?" Wendy said. "Me, too."

Together they began chanting in slow, spooky voices:

Once upon a midnight dreary,
While I pondered weak and weary . . .

"Don't start that creepy stuff," Michael begged.

"Speaking of creepy," Trent said, "did you meet the writer they call The Stroller?"

"No," said Michael, turning and looking back into the room. "Which one?"

"I don't know," said Trent. "I kept hearing the name but I couldn't tell which one could be him."

"Or her," Stacy added.

"Sure," said Trent. "Or anybody. If he or she were even there at all. And something else is sort of strange," Trent added looking at Stacy.

"What?" asked Wendy.

Trent didn't say anything. He just kept staring at Stacy.

"Well, *what* for heaven's sake?" Wendy repeated.

"Stacy's mom keeps going up to the writers and whispering something," Trent said.

"Don't you compare my mom to any weird writers," Stacy said, balling up her fist.

"Whoa," said Trent, taking a step back. "I didn't mean she was weird, too. I just meant that seemed strange."

"Maybe it has something to do with what we overheard at the dairy bar today," Michael said.

"Aw, they were just kidding," Wendy assured them. "Mother likes to do that. Right, Michael?"

"Yeah," said Michael. "She's always teasing us."

"Well, there are some people I know here, and they're real nice," Stacy said, to change the subject. "Bob Terrell writes funny things for the Asheville newspaper."

"I saw Jim McAllister," said Wendy. "I recognized him from his picture in the Greenville paper Dad brings home every night."

"And good old Kevin McKee with *PM Magazine*," Michael added.

Stacy rubbed her chin. "If I were writing a mystery it would be about a bunch of weird mystery writers getting in a mystery."

"Yeah," said Michael. "But remember — you're not a writer."

Just then Ms. Brown motioned for the kids to join her. They wandered through the dimly lit room around the old-fashioned wooden furniture to where she was talking to another writer. Just as they walked up she put one finger to her lips. "Now, remember," she said to the writer, "Don't say a word!"

6
NO PIECES TO PLAY WITH

All the way to Biltmore House they whispered and wondered what the man who looked like Edgar Allan Poe was not supposed to tell anyone. But by the time they got to Biltmore House, it was too late. Everyone else knew, and that was all they talked about.

The house looked spooky in the moonlight. One of the tall pointed spires stuck right up into the fat, round moon as though it would burst it. Stacy felt sure that any minute she would see a witch on a broomstick whiz by.

Moonlight flickered across the manes of the stone lions guarding the front door. They looked like they would sneak forward at any time and gobble them up.

The closer they got to the house, the larger it seemed. Stacy looked up. All she could see was the house — walls and windows and roof and spires.

When they were inside the children gasped. "It's like a church," Trent whispered. Down one side they could see a long room with what looked like one sitting area after another. In the other direction was the Winter Garden.

The Winter Garden was a sunken room that you could enter from several arched doorways. Overhead, a round dome of windows peered out into the night sky like a big eye. The moon spied down upon them. Heavy-looking iron and glass lanterns hung down into the room and the lights were very low.

Stacy figured it was called the Winter Garden because of all the palms and flowers and ferns that filled the room. She didn't know whether she felt more like she was on a Hollywood movie set or taking an indoor jungle safari.

The kids had wandered into the Winter Garden with the adults and found themselves standing next to a strange-looking mystery writer. He leaned over and whispered mysteriously, "There's a trap door in the floor."

Stacy jumped first on one foot and then the other. But she couldn't figure out what good that would do so she just stood still and felt her legs quiver. Was that the floor moving or her knees, she wondered?

"I don't believe it," Wendy whispered.

Michael and Trent just stood frozen like the statue atop the fountain in the middle of the room.

Another writer had overheard them and said, "There really is a trap door, you know. They use it to bring plants up from the storeroom in the basement."

"Why don't they just bring them in through the front door?" asked Michael. "It's sure big enough," he added with a laugh.

The curly-headed lady giggled like a little girl. "For the same reason you don't see a clothesline outdoors," she said.

"I think she means that isn't very swanky," Wendy said with a sigh.

"They probably don't even have anything here as ordinary as garbage."

"Yeah," said Trent. "It's probably not allowed."

"It must not be allowed at our house, either, since I have to take it out all the time," Michael grumbled.

"Why don't you go stand on the trap door," Wendy told him, giving him a little shove across the marble floor.

The little old lady had vanished just as quickly as if she had slipped through a trap door. They found themselves standing in the Winter Garden all alone. The adults had moved to another room and were all hovering around something, talking up a storm.

The kids wheedled their way between the press of adults and discovered them staring at a small table with a game board on it. But there were no pieces of the game to be seen.

"It's a checkerboard," Stacy said.

"No it isn't," Michael argued. "It's a chessboard."

"Then where are all the chess pieces?" Trent said.

Mr. Terrell leaned over and spoke to them. He was usually smiling, but tonight he looked very upset.

"The pieces are gone," he said. "And they were very special."

Mr. Terrell gently patted the small table that the empty board sat on. "This table once belonged to Napoleon Bonaparte," he said.

"You mean the Napoleon we read about in our history book?" Stacy asked.

"The guy with his hand under his coat scratching his bellybutton?" Wendy added.

Mr. Terrell didn't even smile, Stacy noted. "That's right," he said, glumly.

"Well, where are they?" Michael asked. "I love to play chess and a game right now would be real nice."

"I said they're gone," Mr. Terrell repeated.

"You mean someone borrowed them?" Trent asked.

"Not borrowed," Mr. Terrell said seriously. "Stolen — and the set is priceless."

"Does that mean it doesn't cost anything?" Michael asked, punching Wendy in the back.

"No silly," Wendy said. "That means that they're irreplaceable – that no amount could get them back – they're special."

"You mean like my baseball cards," Michael said.

"Oh, brother," said Wendy.

Suddenly, the face of the Edgar Allan Poe writer appeared. He stooped over and put his face close to theirs. "Did you know that when Napoleon died they cut out his heart and put it in a cup on this table?" As soon as he said this he jerked his head up and vanished.

"Yikes!" Michael squealed. "Do you believe that?"

"I don't believe anything," Wendy told him.

"As long as his heart's not there now," Stacy said, looking suspiciously under the table.

"Let's get out of here," said Trent, leading them up a few steps and through a door.

They walked way down a hall until they were away from the adults.

"Look at this neat room," Trent said suddenly.

"This is the Billiard Room," Stacy said, pointing to the green felt-covered game tables.

"Pretty swanky pool hall," Wendy said. The large paneled room was outlined with fancy woodwork from the floor to the ceiling. There was another big fireplace. The two billiard tables had carvings all around the brightly polished wood and sat on fat, fancy legs.

"I think we're being watched," Michael said.

"You noticed," said Wendy. All around the walls were stuffed deer heads and antelope and other animals with soft fur and big eyes.

They made Stacy feel sad. She was a real animal lover. And, although the animals were beautiful and looked almost lifelike, she would rather see them out running around the estate.

"That's not what I meant," Michael said. He pointed down at the polished wooden floor. His toes were inches away from a mouthful of big teeth. The mouth was attached to a large bear rug. The head was at the end nearest Michael's leg and looked like it might eat his foot for dinner at any minute. The big brown eyes did look like they were looking right at him.

"Well, I sure wouldn't want to see him too close," Stacy admitted.

Suddenly Trent waved his hand to shush them. They turned to see some of the writers moving down the hall. "Are we supposed to be in here?" he whispered.

Stacy shrugged her shoulders, and they all moved farther into the billiard room so that they couldn't be seen.

They could overhear the adults still talking about the missing chess set. But they could only hear bits and pieces.

" . . . Reward?" said one, with a surprised note in her voice.

In a moment they heard, "Oh, millions!"

Stacy gasped. *Millions.* "If I could find the chess set and get a million dollar reward, I guess that would pay for my way to California," she said excitedly.

"Good luck," said Wendy. "You don't even know what the chess set looks like or who took it or where or even why."

Suddenly the two ladies moved closer to the doorway. Stacy moved back a step and stepped on Michael's toe. He must have thought the bear bit him because he hollered and grabbed his foot, shoving his elbow into Wendy's side. She cried out and backed into Trent, who fell against the wall.

It was then the paneling moved.

"A secret door!" Stacy said.

Stacy Goes Through a Secret Door

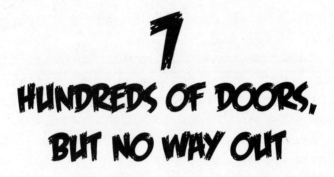

7

HUNDREDS OF DOORS, BUT NO WAY OUT

Just as the two ladies moved into the doorway of the Billiard Room the children slipped through the secret door and into the next room.

"Escape!" Trent said, swiping his hand across his forehead and slinging his fingers downward.

Wendy cupped her hands over her mouth. "Did you see the look on their faces?" she asked. "They weren't sure if they saw us or ghosts."

"They're probably sure enough to get us in trouble with our parents," Stacy said. "And we promised your mother we'd behave," she reminded Wendy.

"Well, when they leave we'll just go back," Wendy said.

Trent looked at the smooth wall. "But how?" he demanded. "And where are we anyway?"

"Good question," said Stacy, looking around the room with its dark blue chairs and bookcases filled with books. "There are only more than 250 rooms in this place you know."

"It could take us all night to find our way out of here," Michael said.

"Well, we won't find our way back standing here," Stacy said. "Let's keep moving. We're only on the other side of the wall. Maybe we can get back to the Winter Garden through another door."

Peeking first, they slipped into the hall. Everything was dark except for a few old-fashioned lightbulbs they figured must be left on at night. For a moment they stood very still. There wasn't a sound. Not even a distant sound of voices.

Where were they? Stacy wondered to herself. She led the way for awhile. Up dark, narrow halls and down a winding flight of stairs they wandered. Soon they were thoroughly lost.

"This must be a dungeon," Michael said, sticking his head into a dark room filled with strange machine-like contraptions.

"Looks like a torture chamber for sure," Trent agreed.

Wendy ventured further into the room. She spotted something that made her giggle. "I don't think so," she said, picking up an iron and waving it at the boys. "I think this is the laundry."

"It sure is a big one," Trent noted.

"Well, think of all the dirty sheets you'd have to wash in a house like this," Wendy said.

"These don't look like our washer and dryer," Michael said.

Wendy pointed at the strange metal containers. "They sure don't. These must be about the first ever made."

Stacy grabbed hold of one of the metal pipes. She thought it felt cold and hard like a skeleton bone. "All I know," she said, "is this isn't finding our way back." She turned and led them out of the room.

There was another series of small rooms. Some had more laundry equipment in them. There was an old-timey bathroom and a room filled with all kinds of flowers. Some were in vases, some were just spread around the countertop.

Michael wrinkled his freckled nose at the sweet scents.

"I think that's where they make funeral wreaths," he said.

"Oh, hush," said Wendy, pushing him onward.

Next there was a room stacked full of trunks of all sizes. Then a row of kitchen pantries. There seemed to be one just for canned goods and one just for vegetables. Another was filled with potatoes.

"They didn't even have cupboards," Wendy said. "They had rooms for their food."

"Look at this," Trent called from the darkness just ahead of them.

He had found a room with a big glass door. Stacy touched it. It was cool.

"That's where they keep the dead bodies," Michael guessed.

"Hush," Wendy insisted again. "You're giving me the creeps."

Stacy peered into the door and saw the glistening silver of old-fashioned metal milk cans. "This is the refrigerator," she said. "There's milk in here and big round cheeses."

"I wish we could sample some," Michael hinted. But Wendy grabbed his arm and tugged him forward.

Next they went through a group of rooms that were very tiny. Each had a small metal bed and dresser and a little window that seemed only to look out at a stone wall.

"This has got to be the servant quarters," Wendy said.

"But the rooms are so tiny and plain compared to the big fancy rooms we saw," Trent said.

"I guess that's how the servants lived," Stacy said.

Next came a big kitchen that had a big black stove. "That looks straight out of Hansel and Gretel," Michael said. He twisted one cupped hand over and over another. Pulling open the squeaky door he whined screechily, "Put your head into my oven, pretty, and see if it's warm enough."

Wendy just frowned. "If you don't cut it out . . . ," she began.

But Stacy interrupted her threat. "Speaking of cutting things, just look at these." The row of knives and mallets and meat cleavers glistened menacingly in the moonlight.

"Yikes!" Michael squealed.

"Maybe we should take one along for protection," Wendy suggested.

"Don't give her one of those things," Michael begged. "Who would protect us?"

"I don't think that would be too safe," Stacy told Wendy. But she hoped they wouldn't be sorry later that they had left some sort of protection behind. They seemed to be so deep into the house with no clue to the way back.

"What's this?" Trent called from the next room.

Wendy looked at the hanging chains and hooks. "It's a rotisserie," she said. "A spit to cook big things on like whole animals or little brothers."

Michael scrooched his neck down into the collar of his shirt like a frightened turtle. He passed them all and led the way through the door.

"Now this is more my kind of kitchen," he called back to them.

They caught up and stuck their heads in the doorway. There were marble tables filled with big orange copper molds and rolling pins and flour sifters.

"Yum," said Stacy. "This must be where they made all the pastries."

"And pies," said Trent.

"And cakes," added Wendy, rubbing her stomach.

"Have we had dinner?" Michael asked weakly. His pale round face shone in the dim light.

"We sure haven't," said Stacy. "But we're supposed to, and if we don't get back the adults will have a fit."

She turned and led the way walking faster now. How was she going to find that chess set and claim her millions if she couldn't even find the dining room? They could wander around this house all night.

Then suddenly she saw something she couldn't believe. "Just look at that!"

"Wow!" said Trent.

It was an indoor gymnasium. There were exercise machines and parallel bars and a rowing machine and a boxing bag and fencing foils.

"Wouldn't this be a great place to spend a rainy day?" Wendy said.

"You think that would be great," Michael called from further down the hall. "Wait till you see this!"

They couldn't imagine what could be better, but they went running down the hall.

Suddenly, they heard the sound of something fall with a hard thump.

"Help!" Michael called.

Wendy tore after him first. "Wait till you see *this*," she called. "You won't believe it."

Sitting there and rubbing his leg was Michael in the bottom of an empty indoor swimming pool.

"That Mr. Vanderbilt was okay," Trent said.

"Oh, boy," said Stacy. "I'm ready to move in right now!"

"Isn't it pretty?" said Wendy. It wasn't like a modern pool. It was made of pale tiles that went right up the walls and over the pool in a curved roof. There were even chandeliers hanging over the pool and there were old-fashioned lights in the bottom to light the water when it was filled. Around two sides of the pool was a wooden platform just as shiny and polished as the floors in the rest of the house were.

"What are those noose-looking things?" Trent asked. He pointed to ropes hanging into the pool from the edge of the platform.

"I guess they were for swimmers to hold on to and rest," Stacy said.

"Well, someone hold onto one and help me out of this hole," Michael wailed.

Wendy ran up onto the platform. "Only you would need rescuing from an empty swimming pool," she teased as she tugged him up onto the platform with her.

By now they were beginning to be a little bit frantic. Stacy couldn't blame Wendy and Michael for being upset. It seemed like they had been walking for hours. They were tired and hungry. "Let's hurry," she urged them as they rushed by a row of small dressing rooms where Stacy figured people would have changed out of their fancy dresses or riding clothes to go swimming.

At the end of the dressing hall was another surprise.

"A bowling alley," Trent cried. "Well, now I've seen everything."

There were two long wooden lanes. Like the pool, there were chandeliers overhead but the lights were off.

"Here's a chalkboard," Trent said, "to keep score."

"Look at these tiny wooden balls," Stacy said.

Wendy picked one up by two fingers.

"You'd better not," Stacy warned her.

She turned and rolled the ball down the narrow alley. It was so dark that they couldn't even see the end of the lane. Silently they waited and waited to hear the wooden clunk of some pins falling. Instead they heard something else.

"Ouch!" cried a voice at the end of the alley.

8

ONE WATCHING EYE

"Who was that?" Wendy cried.

"There's someone at the end of the alley!" Stacy screamed. She ran a few steps down the wooden alley. Tripping, she skidded farther down the alley until she was in darkness too.

Suddenly, a hand reached out and grabbed her. She was so close, but she could only see a dark sleeve as the hand spun her around and shoved her roughly back down the alley.

She felt like a bowling ball going in the wrong direction. As soon as she could get her balance, she jumped up and ran the rest of the way down the alley to the others. But when she reached them, she didn't know which end of the bowling alley was the worst place to be. For there stood her mother with her hands on her hips.

"Just what do you think you're doing, young lady?" she asked sternly. "I thought you kids were going to behave. And now here I find you gallivanting all over the house in places where you're not supposed to be." She looked very angry.

The kids all started talking at once trying to explain about the secret panel. Finally, Ms. Brown seemed to understand, but that still didn't make her happy. "You're right," she said. "There are two hidden doors in the paneling of the Billiard Room. But they're not really secret panels. They were just there for the men guests to go from the Billiard Room to the Smoking Room with ease."

Secret doors so the men could sneak off and smoke? If she tried that, her mom would bowl her down the alley for sure, Stacy thought.

She turned and looked behind her. She wanted to tell them what had just happened to her. But she couldn't see a thing and decided it would only get them into more trouble.

"It's time for dinner," Ms. Brown said. "Follow me and behave yourselves, *please!*"

With relief they followed her back to the main entrance hall.

Stacy felt embarrassed when they got to the Banquet Hall. Everyone was already seated and they turned and stared at them. She was certain everyone was frowning. They had been neatly dressed earlier. But after Michael's spill in the pool and her being a human bowling ball, they looked pretty messy. She tried to stuff her blouse back in her skirt.

Ms. Brown motioned for them to sit at the end of the table.

"Good grief," Michael said as he sat down in one of the 64 enormous upholstered chairs. "My feet don't even think about touching the floor."

"This table is longer than the Bowling Alley," Trent said. He shielded his eyes with his hand and peered down the long wooden table as though he couldn't see the other end.

"If you wanted someone to pass you the salt shaker it would take thirty minutes for it to get here," Wendy agreed.

"The ceilings in this Banquet Hall are seven stories tall," a writer next to them remarked.

They looked up at the ceiling. It was so high they could see windows that looked down from the floor above. Stacy wondered if they had been in that part of the house when they were lost.

Flags hung overhead. Big moose heads and a statue knights and statues watched them from above. At one end of the room there was a fireplace so large that it had three huge openings for the wood. Across from them there were huge fabric tapestries with pictures woven into them.

"This is like eating in King Arthur's Court or something," Trent said.

"Yeah," said Michael, "I feel like one of the Knights of the Round Table."

As they all dug hungrily into their salad, Stacy couldn't stand it any longer. Turning slightly, she leaned over and whispered so that only they could hear. "There was someone at the end of the alley."

"We know," Wendy said. "We heard them holler when I threw the ball."

"I mean they got me," Stacy said. "When I went rolling down the alley they grabbed me and threw me back."

"Wow," said Trent. "Did you get to see them?"

Stacy shook her head. "No. It was too dark, and it happened so fast."

"Didn't that about scare you to death?" Wendy asked.

Stacy sank back into the huge chair. "What do you think?" she said.

"Do you think whoever it was could be the one who stole the chess set?" Michael asked.

"Could be," said Stacy. "I don't know why anyone would be hiding in a dark part of the house."

"We'd better keep our eyes open," Wendy suggested.

"Wide!" Trent added.

The lady next to them put her fingers to her lips to quiet them like they were kindergarteners. The speaker, the curator for Biltmore House, was introduced.

"Isn't that a doctor or something?" Trent asked.

The lady next to him laughed. "In a way," she whispered. "The curator is responsible for taking care of the house."

Stacy was so shaken up by the Bowling Alley experience that she could hardly sit still and listen. It seemed like she just caught bits and pieces of what the curator was saying.

"Mr. Vanderbilt was a 22-year-old millionaire . . . *Bildt* was a Dutch town and *more* was Old English for rolling hills . . . the walls are limestone and are four feet thick."

At last the speaker finished. The writers went to meet in the Library to talk about their classes. Before she left to join them, Ms. Brown looked at each child with a remember-to-behave-yourselves look.

The curator was still at the end of the table getting her papers together. "Could I take you on a short tour?" she asked the children.

They were startled. Not at the question, but that they could hear from the other end of the table.

"It seems like you'd have to yell at us for us to hear you from way down there," Michael said.

The curator laughed. She picked up her folder and walked toward them. "You would certainly think so," she said. "But they designed the room so that the acoustics would be so good that you could talk from one end of the table to the other without shouting."

"What are acoustics?" Wendy asked.

"Sort of the way the sound works — or doesn't work — in a room," the curator explained.

"Boy, Mr. Vanderbilt just thought of everything, didn't he?" Trent said.

"He just wanted his guests to be comfortable," the curator said. "The things that this house has — heat and indoor bathrooms, refrigeration and elevators and lightbulbs — were real luxuries that most people didn't have back then.

"How long did it take to build the house?" Stacy asked.

"It took hundreds of workers six years," the curator said. "A three-mile train track was built to bring the materials here. They even had brick-making and woodworking companies set up to help with all the building materials that were needed. Why, one limestone block weighed three tons! Mr. Vanderbilt even built the village near the railroad."

She motioned for them to follow her, and they walked out toward the Winter Garden.

"You'll have to come back during Christmastime," the curator said eagerly.

"Oh, I'll bet it's beautiful!" Stacy said. She just loved Christmas.

"The house was first opened on Christmas Eve in 1895," the curator told them. "So it's a real tradition for us to decorate like they would have at the turn of the century. We have over 5,000 ornaments!"

"Wow!" said Michael.

"Did you know that only one family in five in America even had Christmas trees then?" the curator asked.

Stacy couldn't imagine Christmas without a tree. "Why not?" she asked.

"That was just a time when many religious people disapproved of Christmas trees as a way to help celebrate the holiday."

"How did they decorate back then?" Wendy asked curiously.

The curator smiled like a little girl. She sat down on the marble steps leading to the Winter Garden. The other children plunked down in front of her. She spread her arms wide. "Oh, there are trees with paper stuffer balls that have gifts in them for guests. There's a topiary Christmas goose covered with moss — that's where you trim shrubs into the shape of something, like an animal. There are Yule logs in the big fireplace. It's kept burning for ten hours at Christmas to keep bad luck away. Coals from the fire are saved to start the next year's fire."

The curator closed her eyes dreamily and continued to talk. "There are ornaments of hand-blown glass and clip-on birds with spun glass tails. There's Victorian candy like chocolate-covered cherries. Sweetmeats — sugar-covered candies — are piled everywhere. There are a thousand poinsettias and barrels of mistletoe and kissing balls."

"Yuck," Michael interrupted.

The curator opened her eyes and laughed and went on.

"There are singing and storytelling and cider drinking and Christmas cards made of paper and lace in fancy shapes. There are candles and a gingerbread house in the kitchen. Ribbon candy and paper chains and **cornucopias** filled with sugar plums and wooden toys. Of course all the treats on the trees couldn't be eaten until it was time to take the tree down," she explained.

"Gosh," Trent said, rubbing his stomach, "I'd never last."

"But no one would argue over who was going to take the tree down," Wendy said.

"We have over 30 decorated trees," the curator said.

"I sure hope we can come back at Christmas!" Wendy said.

"It may take that long to solve this mystery," Stacy said absentmindedly. Then she looked up quickly at the curator and blushed. She ducked her head.

"Why, what mystery are you talking about?" the curator asked nervously.

"The missing chess set, of course," Wendy said.

Oh brother, Stacy thought, what have I done now?

"Oh," said the curator sadly. She sighed. "I didn't know you kids knew about that. We're trying to keep it quiet. It's a very special chess set, you know." She looked so upset that she seemed to have forgotten Stacy's solve-the-mystery remark. Suddenly she did remember something. "I forgot your tour!" she said. She jumped up from the steps. "Come on, I'll show you a couple of rooms you haven't seen."

"Let me get my sweater from the Banquet Hall," Stacy said, jumping up and hurrying across the hall.

She ran to the big throne chair she had been sitting in at dinner. As she grabbed her sweater, she looked up at one of the windows high in the ceiling of the tall room. It was barely cracked open, and someone was staring down at her.

9
ZERO CLUES

By the time Stacy blinked her eyes the window had been slammed shut. It happened so fast that she wasn't even sure it had happened.

She ran to join the others. Wendy must have known something was wrong from the look on her face but they couldn't talk about it in front of the curator. Stacy would just have to be patient and that wasn't always easy for her.

The curator was showing them the Breakfast Room.

"Boy," said Michael. "This sure doesn't look like our little breakfast room at home."

The fancy table was set with beautiful china and glassware and candles and flowers.

"Yeah," said Wendy. "Somehow I can't imagine us sitting here in our pajamas throwing cornflakes at each other."

Stacy was so edgy she couldn't even laugh. Be patient, she told herself. Just keep your eyes open.

The curator led them into the Morning Salon where the empty chess table stood. She slowed down and shook her head sadly, as though hoping it might have magically reappeared.

But Stacy didn't think so. She thought about Mom's "*you've-got-to-make-it-happen*" lectures. And she couldn't even start to make anything happen until she got away from these adults.

"This is the Music Room," the curator was saying as they strolled on. Just as she began to tell them about the room the adults came wandering down the Tapestry Gallery to the Entrance Hall.

Stacy looked at each of the writers carefully. She wondered if it could have been one of them looking at her. But why would they have been upstairs when their meeting was downstairs? It must have been someone else. But who, she wondered? No one else was allowed in here while the writers' workshop was going on.

Suddenly, the tall grandfather clock in the hall chimed. It had a funny, tin-like ring which made her smile. It sounded silly coming from the big, heavy clock.

Still talking to another writer, Stacy's mom came up to her and put an arm around her shoulders. Stacy realized that the tick of the clock, the late hour, and their long walk around the house had

Searching the library for clues

made her terribly tired. Wearily she walked with her mom to the mammoth front doors. As one of the guards nodded and tugged open the enormous doors for them, she was suddenly jolted wide awake. *Guards*, she thought. There *was* someone else allowed in the house tonight!

That was all that Stacy had time or energy to think about until the next morning. She and the other kids met on the wide, sunny patio of the Grove Park Inn for breakfast.

"I'll bet it was just a guard at the window checking things," Wendy said, between big bites of blueberry muffins.

Stacy played with her grits and eggs as the others argued over it.

"Then who was down at the Bowling Alley?" Trent asked. "Why would a guard hide at the end of a dark bowling alley?"

No one had an answer to that question.

In fact, they were all quiet all the way over to Biltmore House. Even the house was quiet, since the small writing classes were spread out around the first floor rooms. Stacy thought she could even hear the soft scrub of their pencils on the long yellow ruled pads they all carried around.

"I have to get to my class," Ms. Brown said. "You kids find something quiet to do."

They all nodded their heads tiredly. But when she walked away, Stacy said excitedly, "Let's go back to the Bowling Alley and see if we can see where the person was."

Trent shrugged his shoulders. "Aw, what would there be for us to see?"

"I don't know," said Stacy, "but we've got to start somewhere and see what we can find."

She turned on her heel, pranced down the hall, then stopped. "How do we get there?" she asked.

"I think I can find it again," Wendy said. "Let me lead."

She trotted off so fast that the others had to race to keep up with her. Through one room and then another she sped. Turns left; turns right. There was no one to be seen anywhere they went.

"There it is," Wendy said smugly.

They all ran forward and tiptoed down the dark alley to see if they could find any clue to who had grabbed Stacy.

Wendy offered to stand guard at the near end of the alley. Balancing carefully, the others crept down the gutter to the wall.

Suddenly there was a loud clatter as one of them knocked over the wooden pins at the end of the alley.

"Good grief," Stacy said. "Be quiet. We'll have the whole house down here."

"The problem with this old-timey bowling alley is that you have to pick up the pins," Michael complained, as he set them back up one by one.

"Hey!" Wendy shouted from the other end of the alley. "Get down here — quick!"

Thinking that an adult or a guard had shown up they all charged back up the alley. But Wendy was just staring at the chalkboard on the wall. "Look at this!" she cried.

Everyone stretched and strained to see the chalk writing scrawled in one of the scoreboxes.

Wendy read aloud:

Stay out of Section 6.

"What's a section 6?" Stacy said.

10

WHAT'S A SECTION 6?

"What does that mean?" Trent asked.

"Do you think it's some kind of clue?" Wendy said.

"It's really sort of a negative clue," Stacy decided. She stepped back from the chalkboard. "It's not telling us where anything is."

"Maybe it is," Trent said. "Maybe whoever was here the other night wants to be sure we stay away from where they hid the chess set."

"But why would they leave a clue like this for us to see?" Wendy asked, confused.

Stacy laughed. "I guess because everyone else is behaving themselves and we were the only ones going around in the house where we're not supposed to."

"Well," Michael figured, "if the clue-writer says not to look in Section 6, I guess that's where we better start."

Stacy slapped her sides. "Exactly," she agreed. Then she threw her arms into the air. "Only, where is Section 6?"

"Let's ask Uncle Ed," Wendy suggested.

Uncle Ed was a nice guard they had met. He liked to tease them. They all nodded in agreement and hurried back to the entrance hall where the guard was stationed.

"Good morning, kids," he said happily.

Good morning, Uncle Ed," Stacy said. "We want to ask you a question."

"That's what I'm here for," he said with a big smile. "To answer all your questions I can."

"Good," said Michael bluntly. "Where is Section 6?"

Uncle Ed's friendly smile turned into a frown. "Why do you want to know that?" he asked.

The children were silent for a moment. They all stared down at the intricately patterned Oriental rug.

Then Trent looked up. "One of the writers was writing about it," he said. "We just wondered what they meant."

Uncle Ed rubbed his chin. "I'll tell you where it is but it's off limits," he warned them. He led them outside to the Porte Cochere, the covered porch where the carriages used to unload guests. Pointing up over the right side of the house he told them, "Section 6 is what we call the old Bachelor's Wing.

That's where the unmarried men would come and stay when they would visit here."

"What's it used for now?" Wendy asked.

"Oh, we have some work offices there," the guard said. "And it's used for storage."

The kids looked eagerly up at the windows to the rooms of section six. The ugly, goblin-like heads of the stone gargoyles seemed to stare at them in a fierce warning to stay away.

"Now," said Uncle Ed. "Just to make sure you characters don't make a beeline up there, I'm going to shoo you in the opposite direction."

He aimed a big finger back towards the entrance to the house. Reluctantly, they led the way back, and he followed. Stacy wondered if he was going to lock them in the dungeon or something. But when they got back inside the big, cool house, Uncle Ed pointed down the Tapestry Gallery to the library.

Then as if he didn't even trust them to do that, he walked them down the gallery to the library doors.

"Mr. Vanderbilt was a real scholar," Uncle Ed said proudly. "The Library has over 10,000 volumes. He liked to study science and literature and art," he added, leading them through the door of the enormous room. "And he could speak six languages."

"Wow," said Stacy. "It looks like you need a library card to get into here!"

The huge room was surrounded with shelves of books. There was even a second floor balcony with a fancy railing around it that had lamp posts. A spiral staircase circled up to the balcony. Craning their heads backwards, they all stared up at the beautiful ceiling. It was painted with clouds and angels. It seemed to tell a story, only Stacy couldn't figure out what it was.

Michael sat down in front of the big fireplace on one of the plush red velvet benches. "That fireplace is so big that the andirons to hold the wood are taller than I am," he said.

"What's this room?" Trent asked. He was standing by a carved wooden door. The carving was of a person with their finger to their lips in a "Shhh" motion.

"That was Mr. Vanderbilt's Den," said Uncle Ed, "where he could read in peace and quiet."

The tiny clock chimed. Uncle Ed glanced down at his watch. "I've got to get back," he said and hurried away.

Wendy twirled one of the large globes in the room.

"Just what we need," she complained. "To be trapped in a library with all these books now that school is out."

"No," Stacy said. "That's good. Remember what my mom said about us finding out about North Carolina authors who lived around this area?"

"And she would take us back to the Dairy Bar," Michael said, running his tongue around his lips hungrily.

"Right!" said Stacy. "Well, this should be the perfect place to do that."

Someone had left a yellow pad on the table. Stacy picked it up and began to make a list. "Let's see," she said. "Thomas Wolfe. I think he wrote books, and there's a big house here in Asheville where he lived. And then there's O. Henry."

"Yeah," said Wendy. "In school we read that neat short story he wrote. The one where the lady cuts off her hair and sells it to buy her husband a watch chain."

"And her husband sells his watch to buy some combs for her hair," Stacy finished. "It was beautiful."

"Yuck," said Michael. "Sounds like a love story to me. How about that marker near our house in Tryon. Isn't that about some famous writer?"

Wendy snapped her fingers. "Oh, yeah. Only he was a poet — Sidney Lanier."

"How about Carl Sandburg?" Trent said. "We studied about him in school and our teacher said he lived in Flat Rock. That's not far."

"Hey, that's right," Stacy said, scribbling rapidly. "Let's each take a writer and see if we can find a book about him."

"Where?" asked Wendy, waving her arms around the big room.

"Somewhere," Stacy said. "We'll just have to look."

"Well, I'm not going to," Trent said. "I don't care if we find the silly old chess set or not. Or even if we go to the Dairy Bar. I'm going to look at all these neat drawings and blueprints from when they were building this house."

"Well, just be that way," Stacy said, irritated.

Wendy was already searching one shelf of books muttering, "O. Henry, O. Henry," over and over to herself.

Michael climbed the spiral staircase.

Stacy headed for the shelves in the corner to look for Thomas Wolfe. Hmmm, she thought, these are only the Ls. "Hey, Michael," she called up the staircase. "What letters do you see up there?"

Patiently she waited. There was silence. "Michael!" she called again. The others turned and looked along the narrow balcony above them.

Michael had disappeared!

11

NO MICHAEL

"Where can he be?" Wendy asked, shocked. "I didn't see him come back down the staircase."

"He didn't leave this way," Trent said, "or I would have been sure to see him."

Stacy looked all along the high balcony. "Well, he surely didn't jump," she said. "From way up there we'd have heard him *splat.*"

Wendy clapped her hands sharply like an angry school teacher. "Michael," she called loudly. "You come right down from there this minute!" Nothing.

"Look," Trent said, pointing up the spiral staircase. "See where that curve is? I'll bet he's hiding in there waiting to scare us."

"I'll just bet you're right," Wendy agreed. She charged up the stairs and the others followed. But Michael was not in the curve.

They stood on the balcony and looked down into the room. Still nothing.

"This is strange," Stacy said turning. "Hey," she said suddenly, "Look! The balcony goes right behind the fireplace chimney and comes out on the other side."

"Neat," said Trent. "It sure does."

They all hurried inside the hidden tunnel through the top of the fireplace walkway. It was dark. But a puddle of light showed them where Michael had gone. "See," said Stacy. "There's a hidden staircase."

"It must go up to the second floor where the bedrooms are," Wendy guessed.

"The way Mr. Vanderbilt thought of everything, I'll bet he fixed this so you could sneak down at night in your pajamas and get a book," Trent said.

"Well, let's sneak up them and see if we can find Michael," Stacy said.

Slowly up the skinny stairway they crept, one close behind the other. They found themselves in the second floor hallway. There was no sign of Michael.

"Where could he have gone?" Stacy said, looking up and down the hall.

"Aw, he's probably just trying to sneak off and scare us," said Wendy.

"Look at the doors," Trent said. "They all have names — The Sheraton Room, The Chippendale Room."

"Why didn't they just number them like at a motel," Trent said.

"Aw," said Wendy, "that's not classy enough for a castle."

Slowly they walked down the halls, peeking in different doorways.

"Look at these beautiful bedrooms," Stacy cried.

The one she was in was painted a golden color with beautiful fancy white woodwork all around. There were big heavy pieces of fancily carved furniture. The bed was set on a platform and a big canopy covered it. There were beautiful paintings and china and golden candlesticks and real flowers.

"This must have been the daughter's bedroom," Wendy said, tugging at Stacy's sleeve for her to look at another room. "See, there's a cradle and an old-fashioned crib for dolls."

"And look at that tiny grandfather clock," Stacy said, pointing to the fireplace mantel.

"Maybe it's just a *grandmother* clock," Wendy teased.

"All that's too fancy for me," Trent called from the doorway of another room. "Now this is more my speed."

The girls ran to join him.

"This must have been Mr. Vanderbilt's bedroom," Stacy said. It was large and not bright and sunny like the others. The massive wooden doors and furniture were dark. Everything was covered or draped or upholstered in dark red felt with a gold trim.

"I couldn't sleep in here," Wendy said. "I'd have nightmares about Edgar Allan Poe's spooky poems!"

"Listen," Trent said. "I hear footsteps."

"Oh, dear," said Stacy. "We'll have to hide."

She looked around undecidedly. Then she spotted the door to Mr. Vanderbilt's bathroom. "In here," she whispered.

They hurried into the room.

"Only one problem," said Trent. "There's no place to hide."

"How about this?" Wendy argued.

In the corner of the room there was a big, round solid marble bathtub. Wendy climbed over the edge. The others plunked in after her.

Stacy felt like she was in some magical tub that might lift up off the ground and float out of the open window and up over the mountains.

"Look at that funny toilet," Trent said. "It has a long chain hanging down with a wooden handle on the end."

"That's how you flush it silly," Stacy said.

Trent stretched out his hand to grab for the handle.

"No!" Wendy said, grabbing his arms. "You'll give us away."

But just then Stacy saw something that might give them away anyway. There was a full-length mirror in the bedroom that faced the bathroom. She could see the tub and their reflection in it. If the person came any closer, they wouldn't even have to come into the bathroom to find them.

"Get down!" she told the others, grasping Trent by the top of the head and shoving him down. Boy, she was glad the tub wasn't full of water. If it had been, they would have been in big trouble.

The footsteps were louder now. They entered Mr. Vanderbilt's room. Stacy put her hand over her mouth to keep from gasping.

In the mirror she could see the reflection of a double hourglass on one of the tables. A hand in a green sleeve toyed with the glasses, then sharply flipped them over. Did that mean time was running out for them? She wondered.

The footsteps started towards them. Stacy looked around frantically. She spotted a small window that went outside.

"Run!" she cried. They all jumped over the side of the tub and ran out onto the narrow walkway that went around the outside of the house.

"It's too high!" Wendy squealed. She stopped dead still. The passageway was so narrow that no one could pass her.

"Go on," Trent said, giving her a shove. "Just don't look down."

Slowly they wound around the outside of the house. The parapet led upward.

"Do you think it's safe to walk on?" Wendy asked.

"I'm sure it is," Stacy assured her, although she didn't feel too sure about that herself. She glanced back over her shoulder. At least they weren't being followed.

"I just can't figure out how we're going to get back into the house," she said after they had climbed another floor.

"Not that way," Trent exclaimed, pointing over the edge. All around them was the blue haze of the mountains.

It would be really beautiful, Stacy thought, if I weren't so scared.

The windows they passed now were too skinny to get in. The ramp climbed steeply upward.

"Here's one that's open," Wendy said, sticking her head inside the opening.

"No!" shouted Trent, grabbing her by the back of her shirt. "That's the elevator shaft!"

They all peered down the dark hole where the elevator went up and down. Stacy sighed. "Keep going," she said. She was sure her voice had quivered.

Slowly they made their way around the outside of the house.

It seemed creepy to look down into the Winter Garden from above. Stacy felt like a pigeon. The fierce-looking gargoyles seemed to stare evilly at them.

"Look at this," Trent said, rubbing his hand over the top of a gutter. "It has Mr. Vanderbilt's initials on it."

"Well, la dee . . .," Wendy began, then added, "*da*!" as a window opened and an arm reached out and dragged her inside.

12

THOMAS WOLFE'S HOUSE

The arm belonged to Michael. "Hi!" he said. "Welcome to Section 6."

"You about scared us to death," Wendy complained, rubbing her arm.

"I don't know," said Trent, "I'm sort of glad to see him." He bent down and rubbed his tired knees.

"Section 6!" Stacy said, ignoring the others' complaints.

"Yeah," said Michael proudly, "and I found a clue!"

They followed him quickly down the dark hall. "See," he said, pointing to one of the doors. Just like all doors in the house, there was a little metal plate that you could slide a card in. But instead of there being a name of a room on this one, there was a sign that said:

You can't go home again.

"I don't like the sound of that," Trent said. "It sounds like we might be here forever."

"Like someone's not going to let us go home," Michael agreed.

"I don't know," said Stacy. "Something about that sounds familiar, but I can't think of what."

"Well," said Wendy, looking at her watch, "you'd better think of what on the way back downstairs. It's almost noon, and we're supposed to go to the Thomas Wolfe memorial with the writers."

"I forgot all about that," Stacy said.

"Another house," Trent groaned.

"Well, I don't think it's quite like this one," Stacy said.

Michael shook his head slowly. "Nothing is like this house."

They finally found their way back to the front of the house. The boys climbed over the big stone lions guarding the entrance. Stacy craned her next back to look up at the balcony where they had been. "I wonder whose footsteps those were?" she said.

A big red and white tour bus pulled up and stopped in front of the house. The door opened and a smiling driver called out, "All aboard for Toytown!"

"Toytown," Stacy said with a laugh. "That's a funny name. Where's that?"

"Haven't you ever been to Asheville?" the driver teased. "Well, that's what Thomas Wolfe called it — Toytown."

Talking and chatting excitedly about their morning classes, the adults boarded the bus.

The kids hurried back to get the last seat. As they drove off, Stacy watched Uncle Ed wave at them. She couldn't help but notice that his work uniform was green — just like the sleeve she had seen in the mirror reflection. She just knew Uncle Ed wouldn't take the chess set — but would another guard?

Before long they were back in downtown Asheville. The bus pulled up in front of a two-story white house.

"This is it?" Michael asked dejectedly.

"Well, anything would be a comedown after Biltmore House," Trent said.

Stacy just couldn't get excited about walking around the house. All the adults had gone inside except for Bob Terrell. He stretched out on the big front porch.

"Aren't you going on the tour?" Stacy asked.

"No, I don't think so," Mr. Terrell said, stretching his hands behind his head and leaning back against a post. "I've done a lot of stories about Thomas Wolfe, and so I've seen this old house a few times."

The kids sat down on the porch steps near him. "Well," said Trent. "We've sort of had a hard morning. Could we just sit here with you?"

Mr. Terrell laughed and nodded. But Stacy said, "Trent, we really need to know about Thomas Wolfe, you know — or did you forget?"

"Forget what?" Mr. Terrell asked, leaning forward just a little.

Boy, Stacy thought, you have to be careful what you say around writers; they're always so curious and full of questions.

Trent groaned.

"Well," Mr. Terrell said, leaning back. "You guys just sit here with me and I'll tell you what I know about Thomas Wolfe that I think kids would be interested in."

"And leave all the dull school part out?" Wendy begged.

"Young lady, are you trying to suggest that writers are boring?" Mr. Terrell asked with a twinkle in his eye.

Wendy blushed. The others giggled and got comfortable on the cool porch.

"Let's see," Mr. Terrell said, rubbing his chin thoughtfully. "Tom Wolfe lived in this big, old boardinghouse when he was a kid."

"That would seem weird to live in a house with a lot of strangers," Wendy said.

"It was sort of odd," Mr. Terrell agreed. "There were always new people coming and going. Why, Tom never knew for sure where he would get to sleep at night—sometimes, that was in the bathtub!"

"Doesn't sound like too great a childhood," Michael said.

Mr. Terrell nodded. "The thing Tom hated worst of all was that his mother wouldn't let him get a haircut until he was nine. So the kids really teased him about his curls."

"Boy," said Trent, stroking his head. "I'd just die. Didn't he beat up on them?"

"He could have!" Mr. Terrell said. "Even as a boy, Tom was tall and gangly. His arms hung down about to his knees. When he was grown, he was around six feet, six inches tall and weighed three hundred pounds. He used to put his typewriter on top of the refrigerator and stand up to type."

Stacy giggled.

"He dearly loved baseball," Mr. Terrell added. "And he was a newspaper carrier for the *Citizen-Times*, where I work."

"What did he write that made him so famous that people would come and see his house?" Trent asked.

"His most famous book is called *Look Homeward, Angel*," Mr. Terrell told them. "It was mostly biographical."

"You mean a true book about his life?" Stacy asked.

"Almost," Mr. Terrell said. "And that's what got him in trouble. The book was made up. But a lot of his family and friends felt sure the characters in the book were supposed to be them and they weren't too happy about it. When Tom came back to

Asheville after he had written his book, they threatened to kill him."

"Gosh," said Michael. "What did he do?"

"He left town," Mr. Terrell said. He wrote some more books. Of course, that experience may have been why he titled one of them *You Can't Go Home Again* — because he couldn't, not for awhile at least."

Stacy sat straight up on the porch. "You can't what?" she asked.

"*You Can't Go Home Again*," Mr. Terrell repeated. "Have you read it?"

"Yes," Stacy said. " . . . I mean no. I mean only on a door."

Mr. Terrell looked thoroughly puzzled.

Stacy jumped up and the others did too. Eagerly she headed for the bus. She looked back over her shoulder. "Thanks, Mr. Terrell, thanks a lot."

He just looked at them like they were crazy, then stretched back out on the porch.

"What's the hurry?" Wendy asked, as they climbed aboard the bus.

"I want to get a front row seat," Stacy said, "so we can be first off when we get back to Biltmore."

13

YOU CAN'T EVEN GO TO BILTMORE AGAIN

"Do you think you know what the *you-can't-go-home-again* clue means now?" Trent asked eagerly.

"Well," Stacy said, sitting very straight in one of the first plush seats of the bus. "I'm not sure what it means. But I think it means the chess set is still at Biltmore House."

"What makes you think that?" Wendy asked, sitting down beside her.

Stacy closed her eyes tightly, trying to figure out how to say what she was thinking. "The clue-writer keeps leaving the clues at the house, so they must have the chess set locked away somewhere there and are having trouble getting it out since the guards are keeping such a good eye on Biltmore."

Michael leaned over the back of the seat and looked at Stacy upside down.

"I'm still confused," he said. "What does *you-can't-go-home-again* have to do with anything?"

Stacy rubbed her head. "I'm not 100 percent sure," she said. "But the thief must have figured that we knew something about Thomas Wolfe and would think the clue meant the chess set was hidden at his house. But I think he or she is just trying to keep us from snooping around all the rooms at Biltmore."

The doors of the bus snapped closed and the driver started the engine.

"Are you really sure the chess set isn't here at Tom Wolfe's house?" Trent asked.

Stacy peered through the smoky-grey windows at the cool white house. "I sure hope not," she said.

"Then I guess we'd better search Biltmore House next, eh?" Wendy asked.

Stacy settled back into her seat. "All 250 rooms!" she said.

As the bus pulled away, the other kids all groaned.

But the bus driver surprised them. He merely drove the bus next door to the Inn on the Plaza.

By the time they rode the elevator to the rooftop restaurant for dinner, the sun was beginning to set over the mountains. Everything had a fiery red glow that was slowly fading to a dusty pink.

As the pink turned to purple and then to the first blue of night, Stacy felt her hopes fade, too. Since they had been gone such a long time, she was sure it had given the thief a chance to get the chess set out of the house. Unless, hopefully, Uncle Ed was still on duty to catch them. But when she thought of Uncle Ed, she thought of the green sleeve she had seen. Uncle Ed wouldn't be suspicious of a fellow guard. The very thought made her blue as night.

After a restless night at the Grove Park, Stacy was up early.

Only there was another disappointment.

"We're not going to Biltmore first thing this morning after all," Ms. Brown announced. "We're going to Connemara."

"Where the heck is that?" Stacy asked.

"Just over in Flat Rock," her mom said. "It's where Carl Sandburg, the famous poet lived. His wife raised prize-winning goats. It's a big farm. You'll enjoy seeing it."

Stacy mumbled that she doubted it. But there was nothing to do except follow the adults through the cool stone halls to another waiting bus.

The other kids were already seated.

"Do you believe it?" she asked as the clambered on board.

"No," said Wendy, sympathetically. She patted Stacy on the shoulder.

"We'd rather go to a farm than Biltmore," Michael said, and Trent nodded. Stacy just frowned and sat beside Wendy.

As they drove along, Stacy had an idea. Maybe the thief wasn't a guard at all. Maybe the reason they used the *you-can't-go-home-again* clue was because one of the writers had taken the chess set. A writer would certainly know the title of a Thomas Wolfe book.

She stared out at the hills rolling past them. After all, the set didn't disappear until after the writers had all been to the house to register for the workshop. But she wondered to herself how they would know about Section 6. Only a guard or the curator would know something like that. She looked suspiciously around the bus from one person to another. Only Wendy poking her in the ribs brought her out of her daydream.

"We're here," Wendy said. "Wake up, for heaven's sake."

Numbly, Stacy followed them off the bus. In spite of herself she couldn't help but stop and think how pretty the countryside was. Connemara was in the rolling foothills on the slope of Big Glassy Mountain. The large white house sat on the top of a pretty grassy spread out on the gently rolling mounds below. It was pretty enough to paint, if she knew how, or take a picture of, if she had a camera.

It didn't look like they could get out of the guided tour this time. So she just followed the crowd, feeling more like a sheep than a goat.

"Mr. Sandburg must have loved books as much as Mr. Vanderbilt," Trent said, as they entered the house. Although it was not nearly as fancy as Biltmore, there were shelves and shelves of books in every room.

"Things are sort of messy, like at a real writer's house," Wendy said.

"Like Mom's desk," Michael added.

Wendy giggled.

Stacy couldn't help but think how much Mr. Sandburg and Mr. Vanderbilt had done and yet in different ways. But right now there was just one thing she wanted to do — find the chess set and get the reward — but she sure seemed to be having trouble accomplishing that no matter what she did.

"Sandburg grew up during hard times," the tour guide was telling them. "His father only made 14 cents an hour, so they really had to make do! Even when Carl was little, he worked."

"What did he do?" Michael asked.

"Why, he swept floors and cleaned spittoons," the guide said.

"Spittoons!" Wendy said. "What are they?"

Some of the adults laughed. Wendy just frowned and listened for the answer.

The guide smiled. "Spittoons are just what they say — things you spit in."

Wendy still looked puzzled.

"You know," the guide said, "tobacco juice."

"Yuck!" Wendy said. "That's gross." She puckered her lips.

"Well, he did have some jobs that weren't so bad," the guide said. "He was a milk delivery boy. And he shined shoes and folded newspapers. They didn't even have books at his house until his mother bought one from a traveling salesman. Do you know what Carl did?"

The children shook their heads.

"He hugged it!" the guide said. "From then on he had the reading habit."

"And the writing habit," Stacy added, as she peeked into the small upstairs study where he wrote.

"What's that orange crate for?" Michael asked.

"That's what he used for a desk," the guide told him. "He used them for tabletops and files and typing tables — even to sit on," the guide added. "Sandburg's biography of President Abraham Lincoln has over a million and a half words."

Wendy and Stacy in the Banquet Hall

"Yikes!" said Wendy. "Can you imagine having to write a paper for school that long?"

"I never have that much notebook paper," Michael said.

"I know," said Wendy. "You're always borrowing from me."

"How in the world long did it take him to write all that?" Stacy asked.

The guide paused on the staircase. "It took him about 30 years to study and read about Lincoln and 17 years to write the books."

Stacy sighed. Here she was about to give up on a mystery she had been working on for only a couple of days. Maybe she'd better hang in there a little longer, she decided.

As they headed for the basement to see where they kept the baby goats, they passed through the dining room. The guide stopped by a chair at the head of the table. "Every night instead of watching television, Sandburg would read to his family."

"I sure hope Mom doesn't start that," Michael muttered.

When they reached the basement, the guide told them that after the freshening season when the goats were born, they would bring them here to the furnace room as sort of a nursery.

But Stacy found herself not listening. For here in the simple house, so unlike Biltmore castle, she had found in the most unlikely place something that was identical — that just could be an unexpected clue.

14

ONE MORE SUSPECT

When they finally got back to Biltmore House, Stacy decided to check it out. Without telling the kids what she was up to, she got them to follow her back to the lower level between the kitchens and the recreation area.

"See these things," she said, stooping down and rubbing her hand slowly over a small door on the lower wall of a long hall. "I've noticed them all over the house but didn't know what they were."

"Looks like a little safe to me," Wendy said.

"It sure does," said Stacy, "and I can see why the Vanderbilt's would have had these all over. But I don't see why the Sandburg's would have had safes in their wall."

"You mean you saw some over there?" Michael asked.

"Yes," Stacy said. "In the furnace room."

"Maybe they aren't safes at all," Wendy suggested.

"If they aren't safes, what are they?" asked Trent.

"There's only one way to find out," Stacy said. She grabbed the handle of the door, twisted and pulled hard. Quite unlike a locked safe, the door flew open. The sudden jolt threw Stacy across the floor. She bumped into the opposite wall with a thud.

"Ouch!" she squealed, rubbing her wrist.

But the kids just ignored her. They had jammed their heads into the small doorway.

Stacy crawled up behind them and tried to see, too.

"Yow!" said Michael, pulling his head back out. "Be careful."

"What do you see?" Stacy insisted, sticking her head where Michael's had been.

"Dark is all I see," Wendy said in a hollow echo down the narrow passageway.

"It's like a tunnel," Trent said. "I wonder what it's for?"

Stacy sat back and thought for a minute. "It's sure not a safe," she said, peering once more into the dirty hole. "But since the one I saw at Connemara was in the furnace room, maybe it has something to do with the heating system."

"Let's go see if we can find out," Trent suggested. "Maybe Uncle Ed or the curator are around. They're sure to know."

Stacy stood up and stretched. "Good idea," she said.

But all they could find out was that Uncle Ed was outdoors. Outdoors is a pretty big place at Biltmore House, Stacy thought. But it was a beautiful, sunny afternoon as they started across the grounds to look for him.

The pools by the house looked cool and inviting.

"Wish we had our swimsuits," Wendy said eagerly as they walked by.

Michael yanked off his sneakers and stuck a toe into the cool water. They all held their breath as he lost his balance and tottered momentarily on the edge of the grass.

"For heaven's sake, be careful," Wendy begged. "I've already rescued you from an empty pool. I sure don't want to rescue you from a wet one."

Trent giggled. "Are you sure, Wendy?" he asked.

Wendy looked confused.

"Are you absolutely positive you don't want to rescue Michael from a nice big pool full of cool water?" he repeated.

Wendy laughed. "I think I see what you mean," she said. Thrusting her arms out, she walked stiff-legged toward Michael.

"No, I really wouldn't mind rescuing my little brother at all. No, I certainly wouldn't," she said. She reached out and grabbed Michael by his ankle. In a split second she had tossed him into the water.

Michael hollered, but he was a good swimmer, and he backstroked across the pool, fussing and laughing all the way.

Wendy laughed back. "Well, I guess I'll just have to rescue him," she said, and jumped into the water with a splash.

"We're gonna get in big trouble," Stacy said. But like the others, she couldn't resist. Slipping off her sandals she eased into the water. While the others were cutting up and splashing around, she swam to the far side of the pool. Half hidden behind the bushes she could see something on the ground. It was a chess set with part of the pieces on the board. "Hey!" she cried.

At the sound of her voice, a hand snatched up the set and board and vanished behind the bushes. Then, from the very same spot, a gardener came around the edge of the hedge. He waved a rake at them angrily.

"What do you kids think you're doing?" he called. "That pool is not for swimming."

Before he could reach them, the other kids jumped out and started to run. Stacy swam as fast as she could to the other side of the pool and jumped out too. She called for them to stop. And they did. But not until they were inside the walled garden.

Michael peeked through the big gate. "All clear," he said. "He must have decided not to follow us after all."

Stacy, water from her bangs dripping down her cheeks and nose, finally caught her breath. "We should be following him!" she said.

"Why?" asked Wendy. "We're the ones who were doing something wrong."

Stacy shook her head, slinging water on the others. "He may be the one who's done something wrong. I saw him before he jumped up and yelled at us. He had a chess set."

"You mean you saw him with a chess set in his hand?" Trent asked.

Stacy slowly squeezed the water out of her socks. "Well, I didn't really see him and the chess set together. I saw a chess set on the ground. Someone snatched it up. And then he appeared from the same spot."

"That sure seems suspicious," Wendy agreed. "Could you tell if it was the missing chess set?"

"No," Stacy said dejectedly. "It was too far away and too low to the ground."

"Yeah, but how many other chess sets are around this place?" Michael asked.

"True," Stacy said. "But we sure missed our chance."

"Let's look around the garden and see if we see him," Wendy said.

"Or at least Uncle Ed," added Trent.

Stacy sighed. "Maybe walking around in the sun will at least dry us off," she agreed.

The garden was beautiful. A big stone wall with red tiles on top surrounded it. There were trees growing flat against the inside of the wall and flowers of every kind growing in pretty patterns all around.

It smelled wonderful. Stacy decided it must smell good to the bees too. She stepped sideways to avoid colliding with a fuzzy black and gold bee in a hurry to the next rosebush.

"What's that big glass building?" Trent asked. He pointed to the end of the garden.

"That's the greenhouse," Stacy said. "They grow flowers in there all year 'round."

They ran through a lattice-covered tunnel. The shady, cool greenhouse gave them a chill in their still damp clothes. It was strangely quiet.

"It's like a jungle in here," Wendy said.

"With something waiting to pounce on us," Trent added.

15

BLOOD

But nothing did pounce on them. In fact, there didn't seem to be anyone around.

They wandered out into the Azalea Garden and down to the Bass Pond. The pretty little pond of water with the island floating in the middle looked even more appealing than the pool. A bridge crossed over part of the pond and a round gazebo stuck out into the water.

"This looks like a great place for make-believing," Michael said. He climbed onto the top of a rock wall.

"Make-believing what?" Stacy asked.

"Make-believing anything," Michael said. He bent his knees and thrust one arm out as though he had a sword. "Pirates, or dungeons and dragons or the Loch Ness Monster."

"You're too old to make-believe, Michael," Wendy said.

"You're never too old to pretend," Michael argued. "Or how else would Mom make up her stories."

Wendy didn't have an answer. They sat down on the warm stone wall.

"Well, let's make-believe we're Uncle Ed and think where we'd be," Stacy suggested.

Just then one of the Biltmore service trucks rumbled up on the road above them. The driver honked the horn. Startled, they all turned around. "Hey," a voice shouted. "You kids need a ride? It'll be dark before too long."

"We're looking for Uncle Ed," Stacy called up the hill.

There was a moment of silence and then, "He may be over at Deerpark or the calf barn. C'mon, I'll give you a ride."

Stacy remembered it was a long way around to the dairy barns. So, as comfortable as it was in the warm late afternoon sun by the lake, she jumped up. "Let's take him up on it," she said.

The others groaned. They struggled up and headed up the hill.

When they got to the truck, Stacy put her hand out to open the door and gasped. The driver was the gardener who had been chasing them. Stacy and the others froze like the statues in the garden.

The gardener frowned. He was young and very tan and didn't really look *too* scary. "Oh," he said, trying to sound serious. "It's you kids."

Stacy just stood there with her hand on the door. "Well, c'mon," he said. "Get in."

Stacy didn't know what else to do. If he was the thief, they were in big trouble. But if he wasn't and they turned around and ran off, they were in big trouble too.

Slowly she turned the handle. The door opened and she got in. The others climbed into the back of the truck with the pitchforks and the pinestraw, leaving Stacy all alone in the front with the man. She sat as close to the door as she could and held the handle tight in case she had to jump out or something. Suspiciously, she looked at the big paper bag on the seat between them.

The man, still frowning, put the truck into gear. With a jolt, they started off. Before they had gone very far he slammed on the brakes, throwing them all forward.

He doesn't even have seat belts, Stacy thought. But how can you think of dumb things like that when you're about to die?

"Sorry," he said gruffly. "I forgot. I've got to make one stop before we go to the dairy barns."

Throwing the truck into reverse, he backed up a few yards to a narrow road that led into the woods. A small sign that read "Private! Closed to the Public" was posted by the side of the road.

Oh dear, Stacy thought, we're doomed now. How many times did Mom ever tell me never to get into a car with a stranger? And now I've gone and done that and here we are heading down an off-limits road into the woods. She had a cold chill, and this time it wasn't from her wet clothes.

They bounced down the rutted road. In the mirror outside her window, she could see the kids hanging on to the side of the truck for dear life.

The arms of the low pines brushed the roof of the truck with a skeletal scraping sound. At last they came to an opening. Before her Stacy could see rows and rows of vines. "Vineyards," she whispered to herself.

Suddenly, the man slammed on his brakes. The truck jarred to a stop. Without a word he threw open the door and climbed out. Now we're in for it, thought Stacy. I just know he's coming around this side to get me.

She squeezed her eyes shut tight. Over the idling hum of the motor she could hear him walking. Then there was a squeal from the kids in the back of the truck. Oh, my goodness, she thought, squinching her eyes tighter and tighter until they hurt. What is he doing to them?

In a moment he slung the door of the truck open. In spite of herself she turned and looked at him. He had a big grin on his face. And his shirt was covered with a big purple stain. Blood!

"Your shirt," she stuttered, pointing a quivery finger toward him.

He laughed. "Juice," he said. "Juice from the grapes."

Stacy sniffed. Sure enough it did smell like grape juice. She got up the nerve to look in the rearview mirror. The kid's heads bobbed in the back.

Slowly she ungripped her hand from the door handle. The man waved an arm towards the vineyards. "We grow grapes for wine here. It's just another way to use the land like Mr. Vanderbilt thought you should."

Stacy just stared at his shirt again and said, "Oh."

16

35 SECRET HIDING PLACES

Stacy sat quietly while they rode back to the main road and toward Deerpark and the calf barns. The cows propped lazily on the hillsides. White clouds turned pink in the sunset sky. Stacy wondered how it could all look so peaceful when there was really this awful mystery going on and her getting scared at every little thing — like a squirt of grape juice.

For a ways the truck raced beside the French Broad River. Then they passed another estate truck. The driver blew his horn sharply. Stacy looked up and sighed with relief. It was Uncle Ed. Both men backed up their trucks until they were side by side.

Stacy rolled down her window as fast as she could. "Uncle Ed," she cried. "Am I glad to see you!"

"Likewise," Uncle Ed said. "Can I give you kids a ride back to the estate? I'll bet this hardworking gardener is on his way home."

"That's right," said the young man. "Got to get out of these clothes and get cleaned up. I've got a match tonight."

Stacy looked at him in surprise. The muscles bulged beneath his shirt. A boxing match, she guessed to herself.

"Well, beat 'em good," Uncle Ed said.

"Aw, you know how it is," the man replied. "In chess, it's the person who's thinking the smartest who wins."

The kids climbed out of the back of the truck. Stacy jumped out of the front. She couldn't believe her ears. A chess player, eh? She took one last look at the bag on the seat. I'll just bet.

They hopped in the truck with Uncle Ed and he roared off. With a curt wave, the gardener sped off in the other direction. Stacy couldn't help but be glad he was leaving the estate — or at least she hoped he was.

They were back at the house and inside before Stacy remembered why they had been searching for Uncle Ed. As they walked down the hall, she spotted one of the safe-looking doors.

"Uncle Ed," she asked urgently, "what are these little doors?"

Laughing, he yanked one open. "They lead to a series of passageways," he explained. "The house has steam heat, and these tunnels lead all over the house so someone can get to the pipes if they need to be repaired."

He walked on and left the others behind staring at the door.

"Passageways," Michael said, "all through the house."

"Secret passageways," Trent added.

"Not really," Stacy said. "Not if you know what they are."

She poked her head inside and peered down the dark corridor. Faintly, far away she thought she could hear a sound. Just my imagination, she decided. It's sure been going wild today!

While Stacy was poking her head down the hole, Michael opened another one of the doors farther down the hall. "Look!" he cried. "A clue."

They all came running. There taped to the inside of the door was a note:

Where would you hide something valuable?

"Shoot," said Wendy. "What kind of clue is that. It's just a question, not an answer."

"That's right," said Trent.

"But maybe the answer is the clue," Stacy said.

"But what is the answer?" Wendy said.

Trent leaned back against the wall. "Well," he said, "I'd keep my valuables in a safe."

"But this is not a safe," Stacy reminded him.

"How about in a safe deposit box then?" asked Michael.

"That would be a good safe place," Wendy agreed. "But that's one thing Mr. Vanderbilt didn't seem to arrange for his guests."

"I guess they left all their valuables at home when they came to visit," Stacy said.

"If I had something valuable, I'd keep it in my pocket where I could keep an eye on it," Michael said.

"Sure," said Wendy. "With all the holes you have in your pockets, that would be a real safe place."

Stacy slammed the door. "No answer — no clue," she said sadly.

Suddenly the curator walked briskly down the hall. "You kids look beat," she said.

"We've had a hard day," Stacy agreed.

The curator sighed. "Me too!" she said. "Insurance! Follow me around while I double check if everything's locked up."

They were tired, but it didn't seem polite to refuse. So they followed her down the hall and up the steps.

The house seemed quiet this time of day. All the visitors were gone and shadows filled the rooms.

One nice thing about walking with the curator was that she could point out all kinds of neat things that no one else told them about.

"Double checking six floors and 43 bathrooms and 65 fireplaces and what seems like millions of doors and windows isn't easy," the curator explained.

Just the thought made Stacy see how almost hopeless it was that they would find the chess set, even if it was still in the house.

"What's that big chest?" Trent asked, as they passed through the Oak Sitting Room. "It looks like one of those Chinese secret compartment puzzles."

The curator stopped. "It has 35 different compartments as a matter of fact," she said. "Mr. Vanderbilt had it made so that each of his guests could put their jewels in a separate drawer and he could lock it up at night."

"So you mean it's really like a big jewelry box?" Stacy said.

"That's right," the curator said, walking on. "You kids wait here. Let me close the window in Mr. Vanderbilt's bathroom and I'll be right back." Quickly she strode off.

The thought of the window where they had crawled out onto the ledge made Stacy shiver.

Wendy had a funny look on her face.

"What is it?" Michael asked. "Do you feel sick?"

"No," said Wendy, "just dumb. Isn't a jewelry box a place where you would keep valuable things?"

"Of course," said Trent.

"And what could be more valuable than jewels unless it's a stolen chess set," Stacy added. Then she realized what Wendy meant.

"Where would you keep your valuables?" Stacy asked excitedly.

In unison the others answered loudly, "In a jewelry box, of course!"

17

TEN-SECOND SEARCH

Wendy ran to the door that led to Mr. Vanderbilt's bedroom. "I don't see her," she whispered. "Trent, you guard the other door."

Quickly, Michael undid the velvet rope that kept visitors out of the room and let Stacy pass by.

She hurried to the chest, then stopped, and stared at it. "Where do I start?" she said.

"Somewhere," said Michael.

"Anywhere," Trent urged. "Just start."

"Oh dear," Wendy cried, "here she comes."

Stacy only had a few seconds to search the 35 drawers. She felt like she was on some kind of stupid TV game show and the clock had started. Quickly she snatched one drawer open and then another. Nothing. Faster and faster she opened and closed the drawers.

"Hurry!" Wendy cried from the door. "She's coming."

Stacy pulled and tugged on one drawer that seemed to be stuck. Just as she was about to give up, it popped open. "Just garbage," she said, grabbing a piece of wadded paper angrily. Just then the curator came into the room. "Stacy!" she said. "What are you doing?"

Stacy could feel her face turning red. "Oh, I just wanted to see the chest up close."

The curator frowned. "I don't blame you. It's very beautiful. But it's against the rules to go beyond the ropes unless I give you permission," she reminded her.

"I know, I'm sorry," Stacy said sincerely.

She hurried back to the walkway as Michael replaced the rope.

The curator smiled slightly. "I promise there's no leftover jewels in there," she teased.

"I know," Stacy muttered to herself, stuffing the wadded paper into her pocket.

By the time they got back to the Grove Park Inn, they all were thoroughly discouraged. It was getting dark. They plopped down on the big plump sofa in front of the fire that had been lit in the huge fireplace. Slowly the twigs of pine kindling began to crackle.

"I just can't believe we haven't had more luck than this," Wendy said.

"*You* have to make things happen, Mother always says," Stacy grumbled. "But we've tried hard."

"We can't give up yet," Trent said. "Maybe we're closer than we think."

"Without any clues?" Stacy said. "And after we go back over to Biltmore for the party tonight, the writing workshop will be over. That will be our last chance."

"And we're back at a dead end," said Michael, curling deeper into the corner of the sofa.

"That's right," said Stacy. She walked over to the fire to warm her hands in the now crackling blaze. "All we have to show for our efforts is a piece of garbage." She pulled the ball of paper she had found in the jewel chest from her pocket and tossed it into the fire. It hit the edge of a log and bounced back out. Stacy sighed and bent down. She picked it up aggravatedly. It was then that she saw the writing. Quickly, she unfurled the note and smoothed it out on the hearth.

She giggled and snapped her fingers. "And to think I almost gave up too soon," she whispered to the fire. "If at first you don't succeed, try, try again!"

But as she folded the wrinkled paper up and she slipped it back in her pocket, she frowned. I *think* I know where it is, she thought. Then she whipped around and said loudly, "But I need your help."

Stacy blushed. She had said the words loud enough that everyone in the great room had turned to look at her. Quickly she ducked her head and sat down on the sofa with the others.

"Help with what?" Michael asked, giggling. "Making a fool of yourself?"

"Are you crazy?" Wendy said.

"What are you talking about?" Trent asked suspiciously.

Stacy patted her pocket gently but they did not notice. "I think I know where the chess set is," she said secretively.

"Where?" they all cried together.

Stacy was silent.

"Tell us!" Wendy insisted.

"I don't know exactly," Stacy said. "But I think we can figure it out. Only we won't have much time."

"How?" they all cried again together. She could tell they were getting mad at her for keeping secrets. But she just sat there silently and shrugged her shoulders. She wasn't too sure herself. How could you tell what you didn't know?

18

ONE LESS KID

When they arrived at Biltmore House, Stacy felt like Cinderella going to the ball. The house was beautiful in the summer moonlight. It looked like a castle for sure now. Like a giant searchlight, the moon lit up the entire front of the house.

She had worn a long white dress and going up the front steps past the admiring lions, she felt beautiful too. The boys were clean and shiny. Even Wendy had worn a dress, although she had fussed about it for the last hour.

Inside the house everything was aglow with candlelight. The guests were in a festive mood despite being upset that the chess set had not been recovered.

Uncle Ed came up the steps from the Winter Garden and greeted them. He bowed low. Taking Stacy's fingertips in his, he kissed her hand. "Don't you look lovely, young lady," he said.

Stacy could feel herself glowing in the candlelight. "Thank you Uncle Ed," she said.

Wendy frowned.

"Where's the party?" Trent asked.

"And the food?" Michael added.

Uncle Ed pointed his thumb downward and they looked at him puzzled. "In the Halloween room," he said.

"The Halloween room?" said Wendy. "You've got to be kidding. How could we hang around this house for a week and not find a Halloween room?"

Uncle Ed laughed. "The Halloween room is a big brick room downstairs where the Vanderbilts' daughter used to have parties."

"Why do they call it that?" Stacy asked

"When you see it, you won't have to ask," Uncle Ed said mysteriously.

"That sounds scary," Trent said, turning and leading the others down the hall.

When they got to the bottom of the stairs, Stacy made a sharp left.

"Hey," said Michael, "Uncle Ed said it's this way."

"I know," said Stacy, "but we have a very important stop to make."

They grumbled but turned and followed her anyway. When she got to one of the little safe doors, she stopped.

"Oh, no," said Michael. "We've looked at all these things. You're not going to have any more luck here."

"We just might," Stacy argued. "Take a look at this." She pulled the note from her dress pocket.

Trent snatched it away and read aloud to the others:

Follow the tunnel to the tussie mussies.

Wendy laughed. "Well, we just might at that."

"And we might not," said Trent, tugging at his necktie.

Stacy pulled open the safe door and stuck her head in. Quickly she pulled it back out. "Listen!" she said.

The other three kids jammed their heads into the hole together. "Ouch!" cried Michael. "Be careful."

"Shhh," Wendy said. "Do you hear them?"

"I thought I heard them when we were here before," Stacy said.

Faintly, far away and with a hollow echo sound, they could hear voices. "I can't hear or understand what they're saying," Trent complained.

"No," said Stacy. "But we could if we got closer."

"How?" said Michael. "We don't know from which of the 250 rooms the voices are coming from."

"Oh yes, we do," said Stacy. "The attic — that's where they store the tussie mussies."

"What in the world is that?" Michael asked, as though he didn't believe there were such things.

"They're part of the Christmas decorations the curator told me about one day," Stacy explained.

"They store them in the attic."

"Why can't we just go up the stairs to the attic?" Wendy asked.

"Don't you remember the big iron gate with the lock on it at the top of the staircase?" Trent reminded her.

"There's only one way to go," Stacy said. She tugged her skirt up around her knees and climbed into the tunnel. "Follow me," she said in a hollow-sounding voice.

Slowly, on hands and knees, they made their way down the dark passageway. It seemed to get darker and darker as they moved along. "At least we can't get lost," Stacy said. "It's too narrow to make a wrong turn." She tugged at her dress as her knees caught it and stopped her.

"What if there's no way out?" Wendy called after awhile.

No one even bothered to answer that question. Stacy doubted there was any backing out of this tunnel. Besides, they had seen other openings. But in the darkness she couldn't see a thing.

It seemed like they crawled forever. She didn't think she had crawled this much when she was a baby. The tunnel sloped upwards. She could hear the others breathing deeply behind her. Her elbows and wrists ached. Her knees felt raw scraping across the rough floor.

"I'm getting scared," a voice said weakly.

"Stacy, get us out of here!" Wendy demanded.

Stacy felt near tears. She wished she could, but she could not see a thing. They could yell and scream, but she doubted anyone would hear them. And the voices they had heard were silent.

But suddenly she heard something else. They stopped. It was the sound of something falling through the tunnel. Something tumbling over and over, clattering against the metal sides. She ducked her head waiting to be hit by something. But there was silence. Then in a moment the same sound again. And again.

"What in the world is that?" Trent asked breathlessly.

"I hope it's not mice," Michael said.

"Yikes!" cried Stacy. "Don't say such things. Let's keep moving." She tugged at her dress and heard a rip of fabric. Oh, brother, she thought, but crawled onward and upward.

"I can't go any farther," Wendy said from behind her. "I'm exhausted!"

"So are we," the boys agreed breathlessly.

"Well, we can't stop here," Stacy said. Yet, she, too, didn't think she could go on. She ached all over and was sure she had claustrophobia like her aunt who got all upset when she got in a small closed-in area.

Her hand felt a sharp ridge. She stretched her fingers out. She felt again. It was a hole! But how deep and wide, she wondered. What if they couldn't cross it? She felt panicky.

"Why did you stop?" Trent called.

Stacy didn't answer. She stuck her hand up to feel the roof. It too was empty space. She stretched out as far as she dared and breathed a sigh of relief. About a foot across she could feel the tunnel go on.

"Be careful," she said, trying to sound calm. "There's a cross tunnel ahead."

"A hole!" Wendy cried.

"It's not too wide," Stacy assured her. "Just be careful."

On she crept. And then she felt another ridge. She put her hand out. But this time instead of empty space it was a wall. Oh dear, she thought. A dead end. She balled her hand into a fist and beat the wall angrily. The wall gave way and opened.

"A door!" Trent said, in relief.

"Let's get out of here," Stacy said eagerly. And with the sound of another rip in her dress, she tumbled out into a room. In his eagerness to get out, Trent fell on top of her. Wendy's long arms reached out of the tunnel and pushed at them.

"Move," she said. "Let me out of here." She crawled out and turned to help Michael. Then she turned to the others, her brown eyes wide with fear. "Michael's not there," she cried.

19

ONE LAST CHANCE

"What do you mean?" Stacy cried, pulling herself up off her knees. She poked her head back into the tunnel. "Michael, Michael!" she called.

Now Trent looked like he could cry. "I'll bet he fell through the hole," he said.

Wendy grabbed her forehead with her hand. "Oh, poor Michael," she moaned. "He could be hurt. Dead!"

They turned to Stacy. "Where did the other tunnel go?" they asked.

Stacy shook her head sadly. "I don't know," she said. "but we've got to get out of here and find out — fast."

"What about the chess set?" Trent asked.

"Finding Michael is more important," Stacy said urgently. "Let's go."

She hopped up. It was the first time she had realized that they had climbed the steam tunnels all the way up to the attic.

They were in a room full of mirrors. Everywhere she looked, there were mirrors reflected in mirrors reflected in mirrors. It was like being trapped in a fun house at a carnival.

Suddenly, in one of the reflections, she saw an arm. She looked around. She could see part of the person in one mirror and part in another. But before she could spot a reflection of their face, the image vanished entirely. "Maybe I'm just seeing things," she said.

"No, you're not!" Wendy and Trent said together. "We saw it too."

They weaved their way through the maze of mirrors to the door. Running down the hall they passed rooms full of only chests or desks or chairs covered with ghostly sheets. Down the steps they ran.

Stacy knew there were times to call on adults for help, and this was one of them. Down and around the winding staircase they ran until they were back in the basement. Together they charged through the door of the Halloween room.

Standing there with a smudge of black across his upper lip was Michael. He was drinking a cup of pink punch.

The children ran up to him.

"Michael! Where did you go?" Stacy asked.

He rubbed the black smudge.

"Down," he said. "Down and down and down. It was like the rabbit in *Alice in Wonderland* falling through the tunnel."

"Are you okay?" Wendy asked.

Michael shrugged his shoulders. "Some scrapes," he said.

"I wound up in the basement. You know — where the trap door goes."

"What's down there?" Stacy asked.

"The wine cellar," Michael said, "and some of these," he added with a smile.

He opened his palm. There in the middle of his small hand sat a pawn. A pawn from the missing chess set!

"Did you find them all?" Stacy asked eagerly.

Michael shook his head. "Only a pawn and a knight."

Trent snapped his fingers. "That's what we heard tumbling through the tunnel," he guessed.

"Of course," said Wendy, "pieces of the chess set."

"The arm and hand we saw in the mirror in the attic must have tossed them down the tunnel to the basement." Stacy said.

"But why?" Michael said.

"And who?" added Wendy.

"And where are they now?" Trent wondered.

Stacy looked around the room. It was so dark you could see very little. But she could see why they called it the Halloween room. There were orange Japanese lanterns hanging from the brick ceiling which lit up the walls painted in creepy Halloween scenes. The room was full of strange things. There was a suit of armor and a red sleigh. A sedan chair like a king would ride in, and an old-fashioned wheelchair.

"I think the thief is here somewhere," Stacy said. "This is their last night to smuggle that chess set away from here. And since Michael found some of the pieces, we know they haven't done it yet."

"But how could we tell who it is?" Trent asked.

"All the writers have dressed up like other writers for the party."

Stacy looked around in the darkness at the collection of false beards and top hats and old-fashioned clothes. She could tell who some of the people were but not the others. "Let's spread out and watch for someone suspicious," she suggested.

"Adults always act suspicious," Wendy said. "How can we tell what we are looking for?"

"I don't know," Stacy said, grumpily. She was tired and sore. And the party was almost over. "Just spread out."

Slowly the kids moved away from her and wandered around the dark room. Nervously, Stacy sat down on the edge of a white wicker chair and watched carefully.

Like any adults at a party, they laughed and talked and slapped one another on the back. She could only make out who a few of the writers were dressed as. She figured one white-headed man with his hair combed sideways was supposed to be Carl Sandburg. But he looked pretty harmless.

One man wore dark glasses and a big polka dot tie. A lady wore a wig hat with feathers and lots of dangly costume jewelry. She guessed that one man with a handlebar moustache was pretending to be O. Henry.

But nothing looked particularly suspicious. Except Michael, who strolled over to her and whispered as he passed by, "King to king's pawn two."

What in the world is he talking about? Stacy wondered. Then she looked down at the floor. He must be telling her to look at someone. And if this room were a chessboard, they would be — she closed her eyes and tried to picture king to king's pawn two.

She opened her eyes and looked at the man standing by a stuffed tortoise. Hmm. Why did Michael think he looked suspicious, she wondered.

Unless it's because his pockets are bulging with small lumps.

Curious, Stacy walked over to him. He surprised her by thrusting his hand into his pocket and puling out a piece of wrapped caramel and offering it to her. She was so surprised she just said, "No, thank you," and kept walking.

She and Michael met in the back corner of the room. "This side of paradise," he whispered and kept walking.

Oh, brother, she thought. That was a Scott Fitzgerald book, but what did he mean? Paradise .. . paradise, she thought. Paradise to Michael had to be football or food.

She turned and looked at the table full with food. Beside it stood a lady. Tucked under her arm was a chessboard. Stacy hurried to investigate. But when she got closer she could see that it was just a book cover.

This is hopeless, Stacy thought, wandering over to the front door where some people were starting to leave. The thief was going to walk right out. People were leaving faster than she could watch them. She looked around for Michael and the others to tell them to just forget it.

But suddenly from across the room Michael cried out, "You can't go home again!" Everyone turned and looked at him like he was crazy. But Stacy felt sure he was trying to tell her that someone who was leaving right now shouldn't go.

Wendy climbed up on a small table and shouted. "Look homeward angel!"

Stacy looked frantically around at the surprised writers frozen in the doorway. She looked up. There was a tall man in the doorway. As tall as Thomas Wolfe. Was that what they were trying to tell her? She just couldn't reach out and grab a strange man for no reason. Besides, he had a big box, and she would cause it to drop.

She looked at the floor dejectedly. *Think*, she told herself, *think*! Then she saw that where the man had walked he was leaving behind dark, sooty footprints. Just like he had been in the tunnel with them! She reached out and grabbed his arm. When she did the wooden box fell to the floor.

Bottles of Biltmore wine crashed on the brick floor. Green glass flew everywhere. Red wine splattered all over the bottom of Stacy's dress.

Suddenly the other kids were there. So was her mom. She looked with shock at Stacy's white dress black with dirt and red with wine.

"Stacy!" she said. "What is this all about?"

Stacy wondered how she was going to explain all this. She saw Michael reach down and pick up something. Carefully he handed it to Trent who passed it to Wendy who handed it to Stacy.

Stacy nodded gratefully to her friends. "It's about this," she said, opening her palm to expose the wet king from the missing chess set. "He," she said, pointing to the tall man half in, half out of the doorway, "hid them in the wine bottles to smuggle them out of here."

The man glared at her. Quickly he turned to run. But there in the doorway was Uncle Ed and the rest of the guards.

The room was quiet in shock.

"Checkmate," Michael said softly.

20

CHECK AND MATE

Then everything was sheer confusion. People were coming up to Stacy and shaking her hands, which were sore and tired from the trip through the tunnel. Uncle Ed and the guards were struggling to get the big man out of the room. People were trying to wipe up the smashed glass and wine. Everyone was saying they thought the man was just another writer.

Then the curator was there, coming up to Stacy and hugging and kissing her and thanking them all for finding the chess set before it had vanished forever.

Everyone stood around her. Stacy looked down. What a way for a heroine to look, she thought. Smudged and dirty and ripped and wet. But she felt more beautiful than ever.

"We almost gave up," said Wendy.

"But we didn't," Trent said proudly.

"And now Stacy can get her reward and go to California," Michael said gaily.

Suddenly there was silence in the room. "What reward?" the curator asked.

"The reward we heard you talking about in the Palm Court when the chess set first disappeared," Wendy said.

"Remember?" asked Trent.

The curator looked like she was going to be sick. "Oh, I remember all right," she said. "But that wasn't a real reward. I was just telling someone about the reward of working here at Biltmore House."

"You mean there's no reward?" Wendy asked in disbelief.

The kids looked at Stacy sadly. She felt like crying, but instead she smiled. "Well, I guess my reward was not giving up and recovering something as valuable as Mr. Vanderbilt's chess set," she said.

Suddenly the man who looked like O. Henry stepped forward. The kids giggled when they saw it was really Mr. Terrell. He pulled at his handlebar moustache. "Well, there isn't a reward," he said. "But there is a prize."

"Oh, yes," other adults joined in. "The prize. There is a prize."

Stacy and the others looked puzzled.

Mr. Terrell folded his arms and rocked backwards on his heels. "The writers' workshop has a prize for the best story produced at the workshop.

And I think that you kids certainly deserve the prize for the best mystery — especially the way you solved it," he said.

"By the way," said Mr. Evans, "how *did* you solve it?"

Stacy and the others began to laugh. They could never tell the whole story, Stacy thought. Truth *is* stranger than fiction.

"Well, I think when the thief discovered we were exploring the whole house," Stacy said, looking worriedly at her mother, "he decided to leave us clues to keep us away from the basement until he could put the chess pieces in the wine bottles to smuggle them out of here. But Michael found the way to the basement and figured out what he was up to."

"And we climbed up to the attic and found out how he was getting them down to the basement," Trent added.

"He had to drop them," Wendy said. "He's too big to do what we did."

Puzzled, the adults just stared at them. Stacy could tell they didn't understand a thing they were talking about.

"What did you do?" Ms. Brown asked sternly.

Stacy tried hard not to smile. "Mostly we didn't give up," she said.

"Well," said Mr. Terrell, "unless someone else disagrees, I think these kids should split the prize for the best mystery story of the workshop — even though it's not written down — *yet*," he added, winking at Ms. Hunt. "For the best plot, the best characters, the best solution."

Stacy thought she heard one groan from an unhappy writer in the back. But then she heard something else — applause! Then someone came up and handed her a check. Stacy looked down and grinned. Even when she divided it with the other kids, she had more than enough for her plane ticket to California.

"I guess I can go home again," Stacy said and laughed. "To California!"

"What is that girl talking about?" the writer standing next to her said.

"It's a mystery to me," another answered and everyone laughed.

"Well, if no one else has anything to say, I think we'll adjourn this workshop and go home," said Ms. Brown.

There was a moment of silence as everyone looked at one another to see if they all agreed.

Trying not to smile, Stacy looked around the room eagerly. "Anyone want to stay and play a game of chess?" she asked.

Now...go to

www.carolemarshmysteries.com

and...

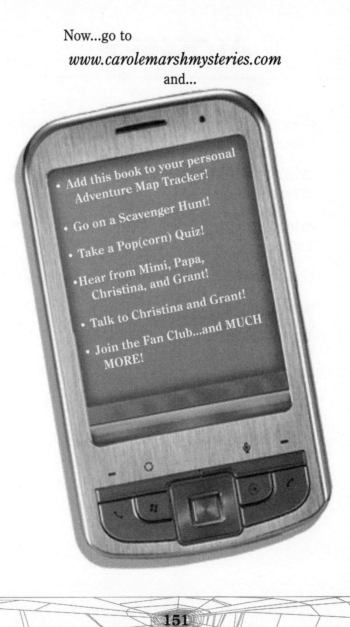

- Add this book to your personal Adventure Map Tracker!

- Go on a Scavenger Hunt!

- Take a Pop(corn) Quiz!

- Hear from Mini, Papa, Christina, and Grant!

- Talk to Christina and Grant!

- Join the Fan Club...and MUCH MORE!

GLOSSARY

chateaux: French word for a large country home or castle

gargoyle: usually ugly animal head carving; often used at the end of drainage downspouts

gazebo: pretty wood or metal umbrella-shaped structure, usually in a garden

port-cochere: French for a covered driveway

tussie-mussie: old-fashioned Christmas ornament made of a decorated cone filled with small toys or candy

SAT GLOSSARY

conservatory: a glass building often used to grow plants year-round

cornucopia: horn-shaped holder often filled with seasonal fruits or vegetables for decoration

curator: person in charge of researching and documenting historical facts and items

meander: twist and turn

mirage: something which appears to be one thing, but is actually another or non-existent; an illusion

Enjoy this exciting excerpt from:

THE MYSTERY OF

Blackbeard the Pirate

1 A STOLEN HEAD

"His head is missing?" Mother asked with a laugh.

Michele, who was pecking out her name - Michele Hunt, age twelve - on the computer in the breakfast room, paused to listen to her mother's strange phone call.

"Oh, I'm sorry," her mother said, now with a serious tone in her voice. "I didn't realize the loss of the head could mean such a terrible tragedy."

Michele listened intently now. What in the world could Mother be talking about, she wondered.

Her brother, Michael, sneaked into the living room through the side door. Michele guessed he didn't want Mother to see that he was soaked with soap and water from washing the car. He was a little short to be seven and had to climb all over the sudsy car to reach the top.

Tiptoeing into the breakfast room, he mouthed a "Where's Mom?"

Yuck, Michele grimaced, even his mouth was foamy. She whispered "Shhh," and pointed to the computer monitor for Michael to watch. She began to type slowly in the rhythmic pace Mother said would help increase her speed. She had started typing lessons as soon as school was out so she would be ready for the drama club she wanted so badly to be in next year. She thought that if she were able to type scripts, it might help her get accepted.

She had seen a Broadway show when she went with her Mother to New York City to see a publisher. Ever since, she'd been hooked on the theater. It just seemed to offer something for everyone, no matter what your talents.

Michael leaned over Michele's shoulder and watched as she typed:

"His head is missing . . ."

He squiggled his nose and squinted his eyes like he always did when he didn't understand something but didn't want to admit it.

Mother came around the corner to the breakfast room. She stretched the phone cord and sat down on the bench across the table from them, still listening carefully to the caller.

She smiled at Michael and Michele and gave them that loving once-over Michele knew so well. She would always stare at their pale blonde hair, then look them both deep in their blue eyes and round faces, like she was looking into a mirror back in time, perhaps when she was their age.

The three of them looked so much alike it was incredible. People would always comment about it when they went anywhere together. Even their bald-headed baby pictures all looked alike. The comments always made Michele feel a little self-conscious, and Michael always scrooched up his face.

Mother shook her head slowly. "Now I'm not really sure I want the kids to come down," she said to the caller. "It may not be safe."

She handed the receiver to Michael to hang back up, then stared blankly out the window. "Bath," she said absent-mindedly.

"Mom," moaned Michael, slapping his arms against his sides with a squish-splat. "I can't get much cleaner than this."

Mother looked at him and laughed. "If the car's as clean as you are, you've earned your three bucks," she said. "But I don't mean tub bath. I mean Bath – Bath, North Carolina."

Sometimes Mother didn't seem to make a lot of sense, but it was one of the things Michele loved best about her. They both loved words. But her Mother, who ran a small advertising agency and could write a perfect sentence, always talked in twists and turns.